08/06/2018

# Quietly Occupied

## Rose Miller

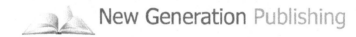 New Generation Publishing

# JUNE 1940

# NORMANDY

# Riverside

Just a few more to go. She stood by the open door of the laundry room, rubbing aching wrists and blanched hands as her gaze travelled over the familiar features of the ragged garden. Hens clucked, pecking at mounds of soil earthed up under leggy potato plants, blackbirds trilled in the overgrown apple trees. Minou had taken possession of the sun-warmed kitchen doorstep, grooming white paws, her grey tail twitching in contentment.

Best to get it over and done with. Pushing damp strands of dark hair behind her ears, she plunged her hands back into the soap-rimmed tub, pummelling the contents with a renewed surge of energy. Tepid water splashed high cheekbones, dribbled down her neck, a welcome hint of coolness. Slender fingers twisted the dripping shirts into loose cords, tossing them, one by one, into a bucket by the garden door.

The beat of an irregular pulse stirred the air. Rubbing her hands on her apron, she peered through the door again. The scene of rural domesticity had taken on an edge of strangeness, the looming oppression she associated with the approach of a storm. Could it be thunder? She stepped into the yard, brown eyes squinting at the bright sky overhead. Lead tinged clouds crawled across the horizon. Storm over Argentan, she told herself, some trick of the wind must have picked up the echo of thunder.

Turning back to the laundry room, she cast a look of resignation at the galvanised buckets blocking the entrance, heaped with dripping laundry. Whatever the weather, she still needed to rinse out the family washing at the *lavoir**. With no running water in the house, not even a well close at hand, there was no way out of it.

She hoisted up one of the buckets, testing it for weight. Albert's bicycle would have useful for a load like this, the handlebars could take the burden. This time round, she would need to manage as best she could. She picked up the other bucket, settled the contents, squaring her shoulders. It wasn't far to the river.

From the kitchen, a lilting voice burst into song, the swish of a broom setting up a vigorous accompaniment. Thérèse emerged through the open door, sweeping her way, pallid features flushed with exertion. Catching sight of her mother, she dropped the broom, hurrying towards her.

'I can't let you carry those on your own, Maman, here, let me take

2

one!'

Lucette set her load down to capture her daughter in an embrace. 'Don't even think of it, *chérie*,' she admonished. 'I can manage perfectly well, you know that.'

Thérèse drew back, gazing into her mother's face with an entreating smile. 'Oh, but I like going down to the river! I can help you wring it all out and we'll be done in no time. Do let me come along, please, Maman.'

Lucette drew the tiny, calloused hands into her own, gently squeezing them. The dear child, only fourteen and so determined to make amends for her absent sister. Six months ago, now, since Francine had gone off to Paris, and Thérèse was still trying to cover the household chores her older sister had accomplished with ease. It showed a touching concern to help, but a wilful disregard for her own lack of stamina.

She offered up a benevolent smile, meeting eyes wide with anticipation. 'Such a kind offer, my dear, but I need you to stay at home and keep an eye on Nicolas. You know he's bound to get up to mischief if there's no one about.' She shot a glance towards the boy, crouched over the rough ground by the laurel hedge. Peacefully occupied for the moment.

Thérèse swallowed a sigh. At her last confession, Father Benoît had told her that she should love everyone in her family equally. He didn't realise what an impossible task this was for someone with a younger brother like Nicolas. She stared at the ground, the corners of her mouth turned down in a moue, easing into a smile as a better plan presented itself.

'Nicolas could stay in the workshop with Papa, couldn't he? He likes to play with the tools and bits of leather.'

'Papa is still at the army barracks in Rennes, *chérie*. He won't be home before evening.'

'*Tiens*! I'd completely forgotten,' Thérèse responded, with sudden compunction. 'Poor Papa, working so hard! No wonder he's never here when we need him!'

'He's a good saddler, your Papa,' Lucette reminded her. 'It's not surprising that they keep sending for him. At least with the army there are no problems about getting paid on time.' She patted Thérèse's drooping shoulder. It was useful to have an excuse to keep her at home.

'Papa will have money in his pocket when he returns. We'll be able to get some new shoes for you.'

3

'Oh Maman, do you really think so?' Thérèse shot a rueful glance at the worn, down-at-heel lace-ups. They pinched her toes, now, she had to admit it.

'Of course we will, *cherie*. Let's go and see Monsieur Lafont tomorrow. He'll have a pair made up for you in no time.' She never thought she would be grateful for a war, even this poor excuse of a war Albert kept sounding off about. A veritable *drôle de guerre*, * he called it. But at least he had plenty of work.

She glanced at the clouds drifting across the sky, calculating her chances. If it rained, they'd have an extra rinse, but at least the job would be done. She pulled her apron off, handing it to Thérèse.

'I must get going. If you really want to help, you could have a go at some of the kitchen shelves. They haven't had a turnout since Francine was here.'

Setting off along the garden path, her lopsided gait eased into its natural rhythm as she adjusted to the weight of the buckets. The washday routine was a weekly ritual, she'd been back and forth ever since they came to live in Marigny, filling buckets at the pump outside Martine's house, pouring them into the *bain-marie*, feeding the cauldron with clothes, linen, towels. During the summer months she'd start the whole process the night before, Albert making up the fire if he was available. By the next morning the cauldron would be cool, laundry ready to scrub and wring out, buckets to load for the pilgrimage down to the river.

At the château they've got indoor pumps, Clémence told her, 'you just turn a handle. The sinks are huge slabs of stone, with proper drains to let the water out and mangles to wring out the clothes. . .'

'Maman, look, Maman!' Grubby hands dragged on her skirt.

'Do be careful, Nicolas. You'll pull me over, and then all my clean laundry will go tumbling into the dust.'

He was tugging at her bucket, now, determined. 'I've made an insect farm, look, Maman! Here's the barn – look at all the centipedes and woodlice I've captured – and I've made a little house for the ants!'

Lucette took several steps back as the ants began to crawl over her shoes. 'What a clever boy, I can see you've been very busy. Now, open the gate for me, please. And mind you do exactly what Thérèse tells you; I'll be back soon.'

She left Nicolas swinging on the gate and made her way down the lane. The buckets rattled with every step, setting off a chorus of barking dogs.

4

Turning into the Grande Rue she caught a glimpse of bright blue, a young man in overalls heading towards the square. The ambling gait was unmistakable, Marcel Richaud, it must be, with that red scarf, flat cap set at a rakish angle, hair slicked behind his ears. He was supposed to be at the sawmill, certainly wasn't in a hurry to get there.

Outside the café, Odette was sweeping the doorstep, crooning away in that abrasive tone of voice you could recognise with your eyes closed. *'Parlez-Moi D'Amour'*[1], it could be, such a lovely song when it was done properly. She would have liked to stop for a chat, but Marcel Richaud was already crossing the road, heading straight towards the café.

She set the buckets down, rubbed her palms on her skirt. With any luck, he might just have a few words with Odette and disappear inside. Odette was used to seeing her like this, but it wouldn't do to let her husband's friend catch her in such a state; hair shoved into a scarf tied round her head, damp sleeves rolled up past her elbows. She pulled the scarf from her head, patted her straggling hair into place, tugged at her sleeves. That would have to do. Grabbing the buckets, she stepped out with a resolute air.

Odette was leaning on her broom, listening to Marcel with an air of forbearance. Evidently he'd found more than a few words to say. Catching sight of Lucette, her eyes lit up.

'Ah, Madame Griot! On your own today? I was expecting your daughter, Francine, to pop round. Isn't she back from Paris, yet?'

'Paris?' Marcel queried, casting a sharp look at her. She thought he was about to say something more, but she wasn't going to give him a chance.

'Yes, a pity Francine hasn't come back, such a godsend she is, when she's around. In the meantime, I manage as best I can, what else could I do? Anyway, must be getting on, there seems to be a storm brewing.' Better to avoid listening to comments about her daughter Francine.

Marcel raised his cap as she set off again. That self-contained, quiet assurance, the shy, fleeting smile; he'd never really taken much note. He found his eyes following the progress of the slim figure crossing the road.

'Ah, she's a fine specimen!' Odette pronounced, as if reading his mind. 'Doesn't look much older than her daughters, does she? They keep their figures, the ones who marry so young, that's what I always say.'

Passing the *Boulangerie*, Lucette exchanged greetings with old

Madame Dupré, clutching a baguette like a prize trophy as she teetered on the steps. Raymond's son muttered *bonjour*, hurrying past on his way to the *Tabac*. The rest of the Grande Rue stretched out before her, rows of dusty, stucco-fronted homes and shops facing each other across a muddy expanse. Hammering sounds issued from the open door of the *Cordonnier*, Monsieur Lafont, busy today, as ever. A row of boots and shoes lined the shop window, freshly polished, ready for collection. Doctor Menier must be out on his rounds, the house looked abandoned, shutters tightly closed. Finally the last house, the dilapidated brick cottage of Madame Foularde. The old woman was sitting by the window; she gave her a wave.

The track leading to the riverbank veered off to the left, just before the bridge, careful footing required. Their local *lavoir* was primitive, compared to other villages, not much more than a roughly hewn wooden platform wedged against the riverbank. Moss-encrusted oak beams, black with watermarks, supported a rusted tin roof with gaping holes. The only other element of protection was a crumbling stone wall set into the high bank behind the *lavoir*.

Clémence was on the edge of the sloping platform, leaning over the stream, scrubbing. Catching sight of Lucette, she sat back on her heels, brandishing a pair of dripping trousers.

'Pierre's spilled oil all down the front of this and wine – I tell you, don't know why I bother, sometimes,' she protested. Taking in the gleaming white of Lucette's load, she added, 'just a rinse today? You'd better settle yourself on the upstream end or you'll be washing that lot all over again.'

Lucette shook her hands out, rubbing her palms. 'I'm sure it will be all right,' she said, privately resolved to take her friend's advice. She lifted a wooden box from a peg on the wall, loaded it with fresh straw gathered from a bale in the corner, pressed it down. Dragging the box to the edge of the sloping platform, she positioned the buckets within reach. Worth the extra effort, she reminded herself; no more wet skirts and sore knees, she'd found out the hard way.

Settling her knees into the box, she was strangely reminded of the confining space of the confessional. Taking stock of the overflowing bucket beside her, she gave a wry smile. Her absolution would be earned the hard way, through the cleanliness of the garments to be rinsed and wrung out. It would be an enterprise far less daunting than any confession.

She launched a towel into the river, holding fast as it subsided into the water. Clémence was detailing the latest exploits of little Xavier, almost as difficult as Nicolas, he could be. She let the stream of words flow over her, offering a few words of support, from time to time, when it seemed to be required.

'You should be firm with him,' she repeated, as they twisted a bundled sheet between them, wringing it out.

You're absolutely right, Lucette, but that little scamp seems to know how to work on me. At the end of the day I can't help letting him off.'

Clémence took her leave, finally, in a fluster of pressing concerns. Lucette sank back into her box, relieved to be left alone with her thoughts. She lowered a white nightgown into the flowing water, letting the folds fan out. Like a wedding dress, she thought, the sort of dress I dreamed of all those years ago. Never wore. She sighed as she hauled the sodden garment from the water to wring out the dripping folds. It hadn't been much of a wedding. The church of Sainte Marie-la-Robert and a mid-winter chill deep enough to freeze the heart, let alone the body. She hadn't been able to stop shivering in the flimsy makeshift dress they'd got hold of, seams let out to hide her shape. Mother wore a black veil, sitting as far from Albert's parents as she decently could. Albert kept on shifting his feet, casting furtive glances over his shoulder. There was a veiled woman at the back of the church, a friend of the family, she had assumed. Until she heard otherwise.

Enough is enough, she told herself, rolling the nightgown up and tossing it into the bucket. She picked up a linen tea towel, shook her head at it. The gravy stains hadn't quite vanished.

At least Albert was happy to let her get on with the housekeeping, no interference there. Three healthy children to love; surely that made it all worthwhile? Francine had been a trial to her in the early days, but she'd grown into a fine young woman, so capable and well organised. Thérèse, dear girl, had been a blessing right from the start. As for Nicolas. . . she paused, shaking her hands out with an indulgent sigh. At least Albert knew how to control the child, though it tended to happen only when he found it convenient to do so.

She was still at the *lavoir*, wringing out the last towels when the rain started. A few drops at first, then a heavy shower, lead bullets pounding on the corrugated tin roof. A stream of water trickled through one of the rusted gaps, splashing her arm. Moving out of range, she jumped back, startled, as a child hurtled into the building, tripped over a bucket and stumbled into her. Lucette steadied the little girl with a gentle hand on each shoulder. 'Take care, *ma petite*!' she said, 'you'll fall into the

7

river!'

A young woman staggered into view, bent under the weight of a sodden bundle, rain dripping from a mud-spattered coat. She stared about her, breathing heavily, panic appearing to subside as she caught a glimpse of her child. Before Lucette could move, the woman teetered and collapsed, the contents of the bundle scattered in all directions. The child began to wail, her cries competing with the cacophony over their heads.

Lucette found herself calmly taking action. She folded a shawl to support the woman's head, soothed the child with soft words of comfort. Refugees, they had to be. She'd noticed a few, straggling into the town recently, from Belgium or the Pas de Calais, bearing unbelievable reports of devastation in the wake of the German advances. Someone would offer them shelter for the night, a barn or outbuilding, any available shelter. They always moved on.

The woman opened her eyes. Momentarily confused, she drew the child towards her, relaxing her grip as she became conscious of Lucette's warm concern.

'You'll be all right,' Lucette reassured her, 'as soon as the rain stops, I'll take you home. We'll give you a chance to dry off, at the very least.' Albert would let them stay, she intended to make sure he did.

The story emerged later on as they clustered round the kitchen table. Adèle, shoulders hunched, as if unsure of her welcome, cradled a bowl of coffee close to her chest. Little Sonia was curled up on a rug by the stove, Thérèse sitting on her heels beside her. They'd come from Paris, Neuilly district; left their home perhaps a week ago, she wasn't sure. Everyone was trying to get away, streams of refugees struggling to cross the few bridges still intact, roads completely congested. The lucky ones had automobiles, others had carts piled high with furniture. Most of them were on foot, dragging suitcases, wheeling bicycles laden with over-sized bundles, pots and pans, baskets, cradles, wooden chairs. Dogs snapped at their heels, babies fretted and wailed. That was before the air strikes began, she told them, her expression set hard. The *Luftwaffe Stukas* flew in formation, swooping low over the roads, dropping bombs on random targets, everywhere around them, the strafing of machine guns streaming fiery cascades over their heads.

Adèle's coffee, long since forgotten, began to swirl and shake in the bowl. Setting it down, she clasped her head in her hands.

'Don't go on,' Lucette counselled her, 'it's too much, too soon, we can see that.' Thérése laid a protective hand on Sonia's arm, eyes wide with alarm.

Adèle straightened up, wiping her tear-streaked face. 'I need to tell you what happened to my husband, if only to come to terms with it . . .' She threw a piteous look towards the child. 'The poor darling, she doesn't understand . . .'

She stared at the table, fingers absently tracing the knots and cracks in its surface. 'That last time, the planes seemed to arrive out of nowhere,' she continued, 'my husband had fallen behind; call of nature, I suppose. I hear someone shouting, my husband is rushing towards us, then there's this fierce whining swoop, a detonating torrent of fire from the guns. I had just enough time to pull Sonia into the ditch by the road before a blast of heat rolled over us, the bomb exploding close by.' She gulped. 'It happened so fast; he was dead, just like that.'

Silence submerged them like a shroud. Lucette drew close, laying her hand on Adèle's clenched wrist. Adèle continued her account, her voice harsh, broken.

'An old woman, white with dust, appeared out of nowhere. Her hands clawed at my skirt, pulling me back. "Keep away", she croaked, "there is nothing you can do. You can only pray for his soul, pray for the rest of us to survive this hell on earth."'

They staggered on until they came to the next village, where Adèle knocked on all the doors until someone opened up. A man demanded payment for what she was asking, sniffed with contempt at the coins she offered, all she had. She took off her necklace, mutely held it out to him. Pocketing the booty in one swift movement, he assured her that he would undertake the task.

'The priest won't accept any more bodies,' he warned her, 'it's by the road or not at all, you can take your pick.' She asked him to mark the spot; one day she would come back and get him to show her where it was, she insisted, meeting his eyes with a determined stare. They moved on, stopping at farms and villages to beg for food, sleeping under trees, in sheds and barns, taking smaller roads in an effort to avoid aircraft. She noticed that they had wandered back to the same crossroads they'd left some time ago. Taking Sonia by the hand, she took the road to Marigny, this time, in search of a safe haven which didn't seem to exist anywhere. Then came the rain, she said, her eyes bleak.

Lucette picked up Adèle's hand, gently stroking it. 'Think of little Sonia, that's all you can do now. You've been so courageous. Keep it up, for her sake.'

Thérèse was on her feet, tears streaming. She stumbled towards the stairs, nearly colliding with Albert as he came through the door. Choking back her sobs, she threw herself into his arms. 'What's going on here?' he demanded, patting her on the back, an accusing stare directed towards Lucette. Lucette was already hastening towards him. 'Here you are, at last, Albert, I was worried about you.' In hurried undertones, she launched into an explanation of the encounter at the *lavoir*, easing the rain soaked jacket from his shoulders as she spoke. Albert raised his bushy eyebrows, brown eyes squinting with mistrust as he stared at Adéle. His gaze softened as it fell on the sleeping child.

'I'll pour you a cup of coffee,' Lucette offered, cautiously steering him into the room, 'and in the meantime, allow me to present Madame Fresnay with her little Sonia. They've come all the way from Paris.'

Albert slowly extended a broad, calloused hand. 'Welcome to Marigny, he said, in grudging tones. Adèle shot a timid glance at him, cautiously meeting his grasp.

Lucette stirred an extra lump of sugar into the coffee, casting worried glances at Albert as he sipped at his brew. Finally he drained the cup, smacking his lips.

It was the right moment to speak. Her voice had a slight tremor as she began. 'Madame Fresnay and her little one need somewhere to stay, Albert. Just for a night or two.'

Setting his cup down, Albert stood, motionless, contemplating the flagstones beneath his feet. He glanced at Sonia, dozing by the stove, then turned away, moving towards the workshop door.

'They'll have to make do with the shed,' he muttered, 'There's plenty of hay there, you should be able to make them comfortable.' The door closed before Adèle could stammer out her thanks.

# Chez Odette

He was on his way to the café when he spotted them, a young couple wearing too many clothes for the time of year, making their way along the Grande Rue towards the Place Centrale. They were trailing a rope-bound suitcase on makeshift pram wheels. A birdcage balanced on top, the yellow canary piteously chirping. Every few metres, they stopped to peer at the bleak, stucco rendered façades of the terraced houses. The man produced a crumpled paper scrawled with an address. Would there still be a Dupin family in town?

'You mean Pierre and Clemence Dupin? Of course!' The woman nodded, prodding her husband. 'I told you we'd find them,' she said, relief animating her features.

Marcel offered to show them the house, it was worth taking a detour to pick up some news. Though there wasn't much they could tell him that he hadn't already heard. They'd managed to escape, just before the Germans entered Paris, while there were still trains. Government headquarters had been shifted, seemingly overnight, from Paris to Bordeaux. 'We've been sold out', the man protested, bitterly. The roads round Paris were congested with refugees; the *Luftwaffe* were targeting all the main exodus routes towards the south.

Somehow or other they found themselves on the road to Normandy, he told Marcel. Not such a mistake going in that direction, less of a chance they'd end up as target practice for the *stukas*. What was the point of leaving home to get done in on the roadside somewhere!' His wife was a cousin of the Dupins, only second cousins, but even so. . .

'Families need to stick together,' she insisted, gripping her husband's arm. More of us coming, they both agreed.

Marcel said goodbye to them just outside the house. 'You'll be looked after,' he assured them, 'don't worry.' At the sound of an opening door he glanced back, gratified to witness the scene of reunion. As he'd anticipated, the young couple were greeted by Clémence with heartfelt expressions of solicitude and concern. Waving his cap, he moved on.

The café was busier than usual, regulars rubbing shoulders with some unexpected visitors. News of the recent Armistice declared by Pétain seemed to stir up even the oldest inhabitants. He shook hands with Monsieur Lafont and old Monsieur Boileau, ensconced at a table by the door, then made his way towards the bar.

No newspapers again. Odette gave a despairing shrug as she polished the zinc covered surface, offering the usual *petit café* by way of consolation. 'At least we've still got a supply of coffee, Monsieur Richaud. You should make the most of it, while it lasts. After all, with the Boche able to march in and take over our country just like that, anything could happen. If we can't even get hold of *Ouest-Éclair*[2], that's just the start if you ask me.'

Marcel nodded, propping an elbow up on the bar as she continued to air her opinions on the state of the nation. Who needs a newspaper, with Odette around, filling in with the latest. He stirred a couple of lumps of sugar into his cup, gazing through the open door, allowing his thoughts to wander.

Coming back to Marigny had seemed like quite a good move after that spell in the mines. Potigny was overrun with Krauts, now, he'd heard, just as well he'd got out. On the other hand, was he any better off here at the sawmill, with endless stacks of planks, the searing whine of electric saws, the pungent odour of resin sinking into his skin?

He realised, now, what a mistake it had been to give in to paternal pressure. Shortage of manpower, Papa putting in a word, all done and dusted before he knew it. Old Cornu treated him fairly, couldn't complain. At the same time it felt like he was stepping back in time: waking up in the same room he shared with his brother Laurence, his shoulders stiff from the lumpy horsehair mattress, hearing his father's hacking cough through the partition wall, the habitual prelude to a long day of monotonous labour.

He stared at the rows of bottles lining the shelf behind the bar, noticing for the first time that many of them were empty. A bitter smile played across his features. Elise would have kicked up quite a fuss over something like that. He could see her now, draining her glass to give him that special look which promised so much more. That high-spirited laugh when she'd shake her head until her hair tickled his nose, the way she'd kick her shoes off, let her gown slide to the floor.

At their last meeting she swore she'd be coming to join him in Marigny. She hadn't turned up yet, probably never would. Letters he wrote to her were returned. 'Gone off with a German soldier', his mates told him, 'what did he expect from a woman like that?'

'Another one, Monsieur Richaud? Odette was smiling, head cocked to one side. 'Or perhaps you'd like something a little stronger?'

He opted for the coffee laced with Calvados, scanning the smoke fogged room while she poured it. Albert Griot and Pierre were huddled round a table towards the back, immersed in discussion; Raymond Duval and Bernard sat close by, no doubt adding their own contributions. Marcel gave a quick wave, dropping his hand before he callled out a greeting. They'd notice him soon enough, confirming his presence with a gesture or a nod. He could count on a degree of tolerance these days. There'd been a number of sideways glances when he didn't enlist, especially when news of the Battle of Sedan, back in May, got through. As if opting out of the recruitment could have made any difference to that fiasco! He was relieved, now, that he'd taken a stand, saving himself the likely prospect of becoming a statistic, victim of that mad scramble orchestrated by a bunch of old codgers. They should have retired years ago, he told himself, indignant still.

He drained his cup, swirling the dregs, lost in thought. It was Albert who had introduced him to the 'tonic brew', as he liked to call it. 'You need to keep your strength up,' he'd say, with a knowing wink. What a revelation for a young lad!

Albert was taking centre stage at his table, no doubt airing some of his more pronounced feelings about Pétain's Armistice. The old boy liked to keep his views to himself, but once he got going he'd not stop in a hurry. At such times, the morose, guarded features would become transformed, animated beyond belief. Marcel gave an indulgent smile, able to predict the gist of the speech. He and Albert held divergent and intransigent points of view on the state of the nation and almost everything else, but somehow they still got on, always seemed to pull through. He'd been a real friend, stood by him, right from the start. His smile broadened as he watched Albert wag a finger at his drinking companions to reinforce a point. It would make up for a rotten day, having a chat with him later on.

He pushed his cup away, shaking his head in response to Odette's enquiring glance. She turned to greet a new customer, a perfect moment to make his escape.

Albert was still in full spate, Raymond nodding encouragement, while Bernard shifted on the edge of his chair, eager to interrupt. Pierre frowned with impatience, tapping his fingers on the table. There was a general shuffle as Marcel pulled up a chair, a round of handshakes and greetings exchanged. Albert gave a brief nod, barely missing a beat, as he continued to harangue his audience.

'Bear in mind, those of you who are old enough to remember, Pétain was the one who got us through the 1914-18 war. We know that he's always put the good of the country first. So now, if he's told us to stop fighting, he must have very good reasons, that's what I say.'

Raymond was nodding his head in slow, smug confirmation. 'I felt so sorry for the old boy,' he said, 'did you hear the way his voice was quavering during that broadcast? I'm sure he hated having to give in, let alone telling us.'

'Yes, but maybe he realised that the Boche weren't as b. . b. .bad as all that,' Bernard was tripping over his words with eager haste. 'After all, they'll bring plenty of c. . commerce. .'

Pierre puffed out his burly chest, as if to obstruct further argument. 'We don't want the country to be run by a bunch of Krauts! That's why we went to war in the first place! How could you. . .'

'What kind of a war do you call that, Raymond protested, 'our troops lounging about for months on end waiting for something to happen. A joke of a war, a phoney war, that's what most of us call it.'

Pierre shook his head in mystified disbelief. 'I never thought they'd get through the Maginot line. Impenetrable, they said, didn't they? It was all bollocks in the end; the Boche just waltzed through at Sedan, with hardly a by your leave.'

Marcel was on the edge of his seat, his restless gaze darting from one speaker to the next. 'How can you chaps put up with this? The Germans take over and all you do is sit around and complain, going on about how it never should have happened.'

Taking note of the muttered waves of protest, Marcel sat back, holding himself in check, but the impulse to speak was too much to ignore. 'Petain must have been hand-in-glove with the Boche, to give up so easily. Then, to add insult to injury, he let that crook Laval take the reins!' He'd reached the point of no return. Raising his voice, he continued, 'what we should be thinking about now is obvious: what are we going to do about all these Krauts running our country? What. . .'

'Calm down Marcel, 'Albert intervened, 'you know very well there's nothing we can do, after all, we're not the ones in power.'

There was a general consensus of agreement, heads nodding, concurrences uttered. 'Nothing wrong with talking it over, you know,' Pierre said, a defensive edge inflecting his voice, 'at least we can sort out what's what.'

'We can hold forth, all we like,' Albert agreed. 'Apart from that, all we can do is sit tight and see what happens.' His eyes narrowed, as his gaze focused on Marcel. 'Best to keep your nose clean, it's the only way to get by.'

As if by mutual consent, conversation turned to more local concerns:

the state of the harvest, the shortages. There'd be rationing imposed, that was the general view.

When he glanced at the bar again, Marcel spotted the close-cropped head of Doctor Menier, his usual tipple of Pernod beside him. You'd never have taken him for a doctor, Odette was fond of telling her customers. The rough-hewn features belied an easy-going, down-to-earth manner seemed to inspire confidence in everyone he met, patients and friends alike. 'He's one of us', his father would say, 'not like some of those medics going about with their noses in the air.'

Marcel was on his way out when Menier clapped him on the shoulder. 'Good to see you settled in at last,' he said, 'you must have been relieved to wash that coal dust off your face!' A stream of questions followed: the job at the sawmill, his mother's health, and what was the latest news from his brother Laurence? Marcel was always surprised by Menier's capacity to remember so many names, even details of family life you'd hardly expect him to keep track of. The doctor probably hadn't seen Laurence since he was in short trousers, but he seemed to know all about the training, the stables, the trial runs at the Paris tracks. Only after numerous exchanges of good will was Marcel finally able to take his leave.

An interesting encounter to report over supper, he reflected, smiling as he anticipated the fluster of gratified surprise it would create: his mother, pink with pleasure, asking him to repeat every detail, Papa drawing himself up, nodding throughout the account, as if to confirm his own estimate of the doctor's worth. At least it would stop them fretting about the Germans. Perhaps he wouldn't mention those refugees from Paris just yet; they'd find out soon enough.

The firm, energetic pace of approaching footsteps interrupted his reflections. Menier fell into step alongside him, as naturally as if they'd been planning to go the same way all along.

'I've set aside some aspirin tablets for your mother,' he said, 'you might as well pick them up for her, while you're out and about. Save us both a journey.' Glancing at his watch, he gave Marcel a nudge. 'Let's get going.'

Menier's medical practice was still in the same modest end-of-terrace dwelling. The stucco rendering showed further signs of wear and tear, the closed shutters were cracked, paint peeling. A tarnished brass plaque was the only indication of the doctor's professional status. 'So dedicated, he doesn't even see what needs doing,' his mother would say, shaking her head. 'With a wife at home, he'd pay more attention.'

Entering the gloomy lobby, Menier proceeded to lock and bolt the door, ushering Marcel straight past the consulting room into the kitchen at the back. Closing the kitchen door behind them, he went straight to the open window and leaned out, scanning the garden. Evidently satisfied, he shut the window and drew the curtains. With a curt apology, he brushed past Marcel to take up his position by the wireless set in the corner, where he soon became immersed in various adjustments of knobs and dials which set off a protest of crackling static. At last he turned towards Marcel, patting the seat beside him. 'We're just in time, come on, sit down.'

The clipped sounds of an announcer's voice came filtering through. 'This is London. The French speak to the French. Ladies and gentlemen, we bring you the third of our live broadcasts from General Charles De Gaulle.'

Marcel concealed his mistrust, offering a demeanour of absorbed attention. Why listen to a broadcast from London? Who was this chap De Gaulle and why was the doctor making such a fuss about him? It took only a few more moments before the guttural sounds began to take shape. Fully attentive, now, he was drinking in every word.

The French government has no right to call for an armistice, no right to surrender to the Germans, the determined voice was insisting. To do so would reduce the country to slavery. There are many Frenchmen who refuse to accept capitulation or slavery. We've been beaten today, but with better organisation and the support of the Allies, we can be victorious tomorrow.

The dull greyness of the kitchen took on a warm glow. Here is someone who believes in a future for us, he realised, a leader with a voice to move men to action. Through a sprinkling of static, the voice went on: 'It is absurd to consider the struggle as lost. . . Honour, common sense, the higher interests of the country require that all free Frenchmen, wherever they be, should continue the fight as best they may. I call upon all Frenchmen who want to remain free to listen to my voice and follow me.' Marcel was on his feet, fists clenched, as De Gaulle concluded the speech. 'Long live free France in honour and independence.'

Menier switched off in one move and turned to face Marcel, his eyes gleaming. The moment of mutual exhilaration passed. Marcel turned his head away, biting his lip. He began to pace the room.

'It's easy enough for this chap De Gaulle to come out with all this stuff,' he burst out with, 'safe and sound in his London base. Why doesn't he stay here on French soil, getting things done properly? He's supposed to be a general, after all, not some radio presenter.'

'De Gaulle had to leave the country before he was arrested and imprisoned by the Gestapo,' Menier explained, with a patient sigh. 'He was one of the first to voice his objection to the Armistice advocated by Pétain.'

Marcel stood stock still, staring at the drawn curtains, which seemed to cut him off from a whole world he'd taken for granted.

'De Gaulle knew he'd be able to enlist support in London,' Menier continued. 'For a start, this is the third broadcast he's made through the BBC; I'm sure they'll be more of them.' He tapped the Bakelite box. 'More of us will hear him every time, unless the Germans start confiscating our sets.'

'What does that general of yours expect us to do, drop everything and hop over to London,' Marcel protested, in surly tones. 'Hardly likely, in my case, with a brother unfit and parents expecting me to help out. . .'

'I know, I know,' Menier interrupted, 'but there's much more to it than mobilising French troops in London. Let me remind you. De Gaulle calls on "all free Frenchmen to continue the fight as best they may." We're in Occupied France, no doubt about it, but we've not been put behind bars yet.' He dropped his voice, his eyes trained on Marcel. 'It seems to me that as long as we're able to move about, we're free to organise some form of resistance.' He moved over to the window and drew the curtains aside. 'It remains to be seen what form it will take.'

From the gardens, the sound of neighbours chatting, a dog barking. Menier listened, attentively, before turning towards Marcel again.

'I'm going to be making some enquiries, find out what can be done. There must be others who've heard this broadcast, like-minded citizens eager and willing to mobilise support.' He moved closer, speaking in confidential tones. 'We need to form small groups, banding together, with radio operators to get in touch with London. We'll be able to pass on information, make plans to collect arms, help refugees. Active resistance, that's how we can win back our country.' Speculative eyes pinned him down. 'If I can get a cell group going here, are you willing to be part of it?'

Menier stepped back, as if to provide a larger space for deliberation. The silence pulsed with intention. Marcel's thoughts were in turmoil, the desire for action battling with the same sense of cautious inertia which had held him back while others enlisted. The blood rose to his face. Just a short time ago he'd been chiding his companions at Odette's for their hypocrisy and now here he was, trying to drum up a convincing excuse for keeping out of it. The Boche were too strong to beat, they'd shown how easily they could trample the country underfoot. What chance would a resistance group be able to offer? And yet, the doctor was in earnest, no doubt about it. Coming from anyone else, Marcel knew he'd have dismissed the idea as the mad scheme of an over-zealous, unbalanced fool. But this was Menier. . .

The ringing phrases of the broadcast sounded again in his head, echoing like a refrain: 'I call upon all Frenchmen who want to remain free, all Frenchmen who want to remain free, to listen to my voice. . .' Marcel took a deep breath, letting go of it in a sudden rush. This was his chance to support a just cause, against all odds. You never know, it might make a difference. Menier grasped the proffered hand, shaking it with resolution.

# JUNE – AUGUST 1942

# La Crème

Thérèse hummed a tune, swinging the *pot au lait** as she strolled down the lane, stopping to stroke the nose of Médor, Monsieur Boileau's oldest hunting dog when he came fawning towards her. She stopped for a moment, leaning into a fragrant tea rose cascading over Marie's garden wall, burying her nose in the heady blooms.

Rubbing the petals together, she pursed her lips at her puckered, whitened hands, permeated with the scent of the *savon de Marseille* she'd been scrubbing the shirts with. So much more washing, now that Maman was taking in laundry for the Germans. At least Francine would be coming home soon, that was an event to look forward to.

Thérèse moved on, a renewed sense of buoyancy in her step. What would Francine be wearing? Last time it was a little blue hat with a bow, perched at a jaunty angle, setting off her new hair rolls just so. She'd have a new batch of magazines to pour over: a *Petit Echo* or even a *Marie Claire*; all the latest fashions to catch up on since the last visit.

Sharing a bed would be a trial, she reminded herself; Francine could be restless at night, kicking, rolling over, pulling the covers with her. It would be worth putting up with, though, for the stories she'd have to tell.

The best time was just before they settled down for the night. Francine would sit by the open window, brushing her hair, as she detailed the latest events at Uncle George's hotel. There was always something interesting going on, almost too much to cope with. You had to watch your step there, especially with the Boche, Francine told her; she'd had more propositions than she'd care to mention.

Thérèse wished she had more of her sister's self-confidence, her *savoir faire*. Francine would have known what to do on that occasion when Marcel tried to. . . She bit her lip, dismissing an incident best forgotten. Francine was coming; Maman would be happy, there'd be help with the housework, some lovely home cooking.

A sudden thought brought her to a halt, setting the *pot au lait* rattling. Francine wouldn't have much time to help at all; she'd be at Monsieur Lanvier's pharmacy. That horrid old man would expect her to be at work every day, all day long, no doubt about it. How would her sister be able to cope with his constant fuss, his exacting ways? Francine hated taking orders from anyone! Maman was quite right, it was an opportunity for her, a job coming up so close to home, but how long would it last?

From the wooded copse beyond the field came the soft cooing of pigeons. A warm breeze lifted the chestnut curls around her ears, tickling her neck. She gazed up at a cluster of puffy clouds chasing each other across a sun hazed sky. Why worry about tomorrow on a day like this? Giving the *pot au lait* a twirl, she walked on, humming softly. Going for the cream at the Marivale farm was one task she never got tired of. At the junction leading to the main road, she hesitated, cautiously reconnoitring both directions. A couple of German soldiers had just passed, ambling towards the centre of town. She held back until they were well on their way before moving into range; best to avoid unnecessary encounters. Whenever she was obliged to pass a group of them they'd nudge each other with strange words of teasing insinuation she was grateful not to understand.

One more obstacle remained, to go past the Richaud house. Crossing the road, she cast an anxious glance at the open windows. Could she manage to slip by? If Marcel Richaud spotted her it would be hard to escape. He had insisted on escorting her home that first time she'd encountered him, holding the garden gate open just wide enough to be able to slide his hand down her back and then some more as she slipped through. Her friend Yvonne told her not to make such a fuss, that's what men liked to do. 'Just slap his face,' she advised. When he appeared in the lane, again, strolling along beside her as though he'd every right to do so, she felt trapped, too embarrassed to make her escape. It was harmless enough, to begin with; he'd chatted about his family, told her about his brother Laurence coming home. Then he started asking all those question about how she spent her time. 'You shouldn't strain those pretty little arms of yours,' he said, reaching across to secure the *pot au lait*, his hand lightly brushing her breast. She took a step back, assuring him that she could manage, but he laughed, swooping down to plant a kiss on her mouth.

The canister gave a tell tale rattle, her shoulders must have been shaking. She cast furtive glances at the windows as she passed by. No one in sight.

With a sigh of relief, she began to reflect on her more favourable impressions of Marcel's brother. When Marcel came to pay a visit, accompanied by Laurence, she didn't want to leave the room. Such lovely deep blue eyes, wavy brown hair swept behind his ears, a pleasing, attentive expression, even while he was listening to Maman. Not that Maman had much of a chance to say anything; it was Marcel who did most of the talking, while Laurence stood by, an indulgent smile on his face.

While Marcel was regaling them with an account of his 'extremely important' work in the mines, Laurence let his eyes rest on her, raising his eyebrows as if in complicit resignation. She cast her eyes down in confusion, not wanting to give too much away. When it was time to go, Laurence shook Maman's hand most politely, his warm smile winning her over from that moment. As soon as the door closed, she commented on his polite behaviour, unable to resist mentioning his slim figure and attractive features. 'Eyes to warm you through on a winter's day,' she said, 'and probably a warm heart to go with it.'

Laurence must have been at the same school with her in Marigny, though she couldn't remember seeing him before. By the time she was old enough to pay attention to boys, he would have finished his studies, opting to work as a groom at the Château de Sassy, no less; that's what she'd been told.

She remembered the day she came home from school to find Madame Richaud, barely able to contain her excitement, in close conference with Maman. Her Laurence had been selected to become a trainee jockey! Thérèse wondered what she meant, picking up, from the animated exchanges which followed, that it was something to do with riding horses in races. If he rode his horse very well and it was a good horse, it would win. The owner would be paid lots of money. It seemed a strange idea to her; that a young man and a horse could do all the work and someone else get paid for it.

A gate clanged behind her, could it be someone from the Richaud household? Pulse beating wildly, she kept up her pace, eyes trained on the roadside verge, looking out for daisies, wild strawberries, anything to distract her from thoughts of pursuit. The steady beat of boots trailed behind her, someone must be going her way. Marcel would have called out by now, forcing her to stop and listen to some nonsense or other. After a swift backwards glimpse, she hurried on a few paces, her heart turning somersaults in her throat. Was Laurence going to follow her all the way to the farm? She took a deep breath, deliberately slowing down. No reason to hurry. Think of the song she was singing with Maman last night, that would distract her. Thérèse swung the *pot au lait*, humming as she walked along. Gaining confidence, she began to let her quavering voice softly shape the words.

*'J'ai descendu dans mon jardin,*
*Pour y cueillir le romarin. . .'*

A resonant bass took up the refrain, with gusto:
*Gentil coqu'licot Mesdames*
*Gentil coqu'licot nouveau!'* *

He fell into step, strolling alongside her, laughed, in a most comfortable, companionable way, as though they had always met like this. She feigned surprise, worried that her flushed face would betray her, but he was drawing her attention to something else, pointing towards the cob nut tree.

'Look, isn't that a black redstart? He's got a worm in his beak, going back to his nest, what do you think?' After that it felt easy and safe to chat with him about almost anything.

Monsieur Marivale, pipe in hand, was leaning on the five bar gate as they arrived. Laurence greeted him with enthusiasm, showering him with enquiries about cattle, the state of the crops, the weather; the old farmer soon responded with his latest grievances. He waved his pipe towards the white flags positioned in the field across the road, embarking on a lengthy account to explain why there were there; something to do with scouts from the German army. 'Requisitions,' he kept on saying, 'will there ever be an end to it?'

Murmuring apologies, Thérèse slipped away, leaving Laurence to listen to the tale of Monsieur Marivale's best mare having to be put down; she'd heard that one a few times already. She picked her way across the manure strewn yard towards the farm kitchen. Careful now, don't fall, she told herself: what an idiot she'd look if she tripped up, went sprawling in the mud.

Madame Marivale stood at the open door of the kitchen, staring at Laurence without the slightest attempt to disguise her curiosity. She turned towards Thérèse with a knowing smile. 'You're later than usual, aren't you? Can't say I blame you; lovely day for taking your time, especially when you've got a charming companion!' She gestured towards the men. 'That must be Madame Richaud's youngest; let me think, what was his name?'

'Laurence,' Thérèse responded in a monotone. She cast her eyes down, feeling the heat rise to her cheeks again. What a fool she'd been to let him come along with her. Madame Marivale would tell everyone, she just knew it.

'Of course, it was on the tip of my tongue,' Madame Marivale responded, leading the way into the dairy. 'What a fine young man he's grown into! I can remember him as a lad, trailing along behind his brother, the two of them into mischief as likely as not; you should have

23

seen them shimmying up my cherry trees to pick the fruit the moment they thought my back was turned. . .'

Thérèse watched Madame Marivale pouring cream into the pot as she launched into her usual monologue. Let her carry on long enough and there was a good chance she'd move on to another topic.

'There you are.' The cream jug grated on the stone counter. 'You're not going to need eggs, this time, are you? Just as well,' she continued, anticipating the reply. 'You'll never guess, my dear, but that rampaging fox, what got at the hens before Whitsun has been at it again, I can hardly believe it, after Guy dug those stakes in over a metre deep to bury the wire and patched up all the holes in it good as new. What a sight to greet us first thing this morning: three hens demolished, one missing, feathers as thick as snow drifts; I've stuffed a couple of pillows, so far, and there's as much again to gather up, if I ever have a moment to spare. And now wouldn't you know our dear Geraldine has gone and produced her litter at least a fortnight early, lovely little things they are, I'll show you next week, only just now I've got my hands full, what with the tomato plants growing leggy in the pots, desperate to be planted out and the weeds shooting up faster than cabbages, I can't seem to get nearly enough done. We've managed to keep Geraldine out of sight, but with a whole litter of squealing little piglets I don't see how we're going to go on like this. Once the Boche get wind of the litter they'll be helping themselves. A couple of them stopped by just the other day asking the way to St. Just, it was perfectly obvious they were just reconnoitring, I saw them looking around, eyeing up the potential. Guy tells me it's called 'requisitions', when they take our produce, more like thieving to my mind, helping yourself to anything you happen to fancy.'

She shook her head, becoming aware that Thérèse was struggling to secure the lid of the canister. 'You never could get the knack of it, Thérèse; never mind, I'll sort it out for you.' She pushed the metal lid down, clamping it shut. 'I can tell you, those Germans won't get away with any nonsense around here, not if I can help it.' Taking up the edge of her apron, she wiped round the lid of the pot with an air of serious concentration. 'We're well off here, you know, compared to the folks at St. Foy, what went on there doesn't bear thinking of and I'm not just talking about requisitions.'

'What do you mean?' Thérèse asked, sensing the threat of unknown perils.

Madame Marivale drew her breath in, shook her head, continued as

24

if she hadn't heard.

'It's time there was an end to it, that's all I can say. We used to tell each other it couldn't last, didn't we? The Germans don't have the stamina of our own troops, we said, but it looks as though they've had all the luck and more, otherwise we wouldn't have let them take over, would we? First we scare them off and the next day they're running the country. Who knows how much longer they'll be helping themselves to everything we've got!'

Standing in the doorway, Thérèse cast an anxious glance at Laurence, reassured to see him shaking hands with Monsieur Marivale at last.

'*Bonsoir*, Laurence!' Madame Marivale stepped forward, flapping her arms like wet towels on a line. Thérèse cringed with embarrassment.

Laurence waved his cap, perfectly at ease as he called out, '*Bonsoir, Madame*! Is the young lady ready to go? Or can't you spare her?'

She chuckled with delight, patting Thérèse on the shoulder. 'Run along now, my dear, we'll have a proper chat next time. I can see you've got better things to do than listen to me ranting on. Give my best regards to your mother, won't you?'

The return journey was almost uncomfortable, the ease of their earlier encounter lost in transit. Laurence stepped aside from time to time, fitfully coughing, then striding out as though he'd forgotten her presence. Thérèse lagged behind, disconsolate, tongue-tied, embarrassed by the suggestive remarks made by Madame Marivale. The lid of the canister rattled: loose, again, despite well-intended intervention. She kept her eyes on the rough ground, fearful of tripping up.

As they turned into the lane behind the house, Laurence seemed to revive. He strolled along beside her, again, to launch into anecdotes about his work.

'I was in the stables at Saint-Lô, sweeping out the stalls one day, when I see this smart looking chap leading his mount up to the stable door; a fine looking chestnut stallion, more than a cut above the usual, you could just tell. "I'd like you to take her in hand, young man", he says, "my groom's off sick and there's no one else about. Just brush her down and make sure she gets a good feed, would you?" I knew exactly what to do, of course, and soon he was able to wander off to have chat with his mates, perfectly reassured. When I reported back to him, job all done, he seemed to be quite content, only then he started cross examining me. How long had I been there? Who was I working with? We fell into conversation, one thing led to another, you know how it is.

A couple of months later I was training to become one of his jockeys, one of the top boys on the job. What a promotion, eh!'

She was able to sound impressed, genuinely awestruck by his anecdote. It seemed like another world, remote from anything within her experience.

He was planning to resume his training, once the war was over; it was bound to finish soon. Longchamp, Auteuil, he'd be there, without a doubt. Just a bit of a chest infection for the moment holding him back. In the meantime there was plenty to do around here and his poor Maman certainly needed all the help she could get.

The garden gate swung open for her, Laurence smiled as he gestured her through. 'Until next time, then.' He kept his eyes trained on her as he backed away. Just out of sight, she heard him take up the refrain of her song again, whistling down the lane.

'*Gentil coqu'licot nouveau! Gentil coqu'licot!*'

At supper, Maman had to ask her more than once to pass the salt.

# In The Workshop

The door was jammed again. Usual problem, with all the rain they'd had lately. Marcel leaned into it, pushed hard. The oak door shuddered, giving way, scraped the flagstones, setting the bell jangling. Albert liked to have plenty of warning when he had visitors. 'You never know who might turn up besides the regular clients', he'd point out, 'Kroger could send a scout round any time to check out the goods.'

Marcel wrinkled his nose as the pungent reek of tannin rolled towards him. Any German showing up here would need to have rather specialised interests.

Albert was wrestling with a cured hide, dragging it from the heap piled up in the corner. Marcel gave him a hand, hauling it onto the workbench, earning a nod and a satisfied grunt from his friend.

Nothing seemed to have changed since his last visit. Marcel watched Albert going through the familiar rituals, running his palm across the hide, rubbing the corners between tannin stained fingers. That little escapade with Thérèse never got any further. Just as well.

'Not a bad lot, all in all,' the old boy pronounced. He nodded his head with an air of satisfaction. Marcel rubbed at the hide, pinching it at both ends. A stale crust of rye bread, that's what it reminded him of. He couldn't resist speaking out.

'Have you seen this? Thin as moleskin here, other end thick as a doormat. You should send it back.'

Albert frowned, while his hands continued to rub and pinch the hide, as though it might become transformed by his touch.

'They probably think they can get away with it.' Marcel continued, 'ever since the Germans took over, standards have been slipping. Why bother, they're thinking, with the Krauts in control, reaping the benefits. Trouble is, the rest of us are the ones that end up having to put up with botched jobs.'

Albert was twisting the end of another hide between his fingers, pre-occupied. 'He's probably got his lad Hubert helping him again. Always trying it on, that boy, he thinks I won't notice. The number of times I've complained. . . ' His head shook in resignation.

'Hubert! No wonder. I could sort him out for you, no problem.' Marcel pictured the confrontation, the dim-witted expression of astonishment, the pathetic excuses, the embarrassment. He'd never liked the sneaky bloke.

Albert stepped back, rubbing his hands on an apron streaked with tar. He scowled at Marcel.

'All very well for you, coming along with a you should do this and you should do that, what do you know about the situation? Raymond Duval is an old friend of mine, knows your father pretty well, too, if you care to remember. He's always been fair, given me good value for money. I can't sound off the handle because his son's not up to scratch.' He tapped at the hide, impatiently. 'Maybe the lad didn't notice the flaw in this one. It's nowhere as bad as you make out, not for the parts I need to use, anyway.'

Marcel glowered at a newly padded halter hanging on the wall. He gave a sigh of resignation, reluctant to abandon the prospect of revenge.

'Well, you just let me know, Albert, anytime you want me to have a few words in confidence with that chap, know what I mean?' Albert grunted his assent, rolling up the hide.

They fell into the rhythm of the work, rolling and stacking the rest of the hides in silence, piling up wads of hessian beside them, bags of wadding in the corner. Once they'd finished, Albert sank onto the *billot.*\* He pulled out his tabac gris, waved it towards Marcel. A clear signal to remain, at any rate.

Marcel stationed himself at one end of the workbench, his usual spot. Smoke began to coil round them. Sounds drifted through from the kitchen, the muted clatter of pots and pans, the cadence of women's voices calling out. He cast an anxious glance at the communicating door, catching his breath. What if Thérèse happened to venture in? A waft of tannin filled his lungs, offering timely reassurance. She'd give the place a wide berth if she had any sense.

It was Lucette, after all, who appeared in the doorway, bearing a tray with two steaming cups. 'My little spy told me you had a visitor, Albert.' She smiled politely at Marcel as she set the tray down. 'Good evening, Monsieur Richaud. I thought it must be you.' Did her voice have a slight edge to it?

'That's very kind of you Madame Griot. Thanks very much.' He hoped the formal constraint of his manner would provide reassurance.

Albert gave a contemptuous snort. 'That boy of mine never misses a trick, does he? Nicolas big ears, I call him. Pressed up against keyholes and doors so much it's a wonder he doesn't get stuck to them.'

'Just as well we weren't divulging secrets, then,' said Marcel, in light-hearted mode. Albert didn't respond.

Lucette laugh, softly, then gave a sniff, wrinkling her nose. 'Must get on with the soup, excuse me,' she murmured to the room. 'Do give Madame Richaud my best regards, won't you?' The door closed firmly behind her.

Albert gazed into space after she'd gone, cigarette ash drifting from hardened, heat scorched fingers. Taking one last drag, he crushed the remains on the flagstones. Heaving himself into an upright position, he groped for a bottle on the shelf behind them, pouring a generous dollop into each of their cups.

The mellow pungency of coffee and Calvados began to compete with the tannin. Marcel settled himself onto the workbench; he was looking forward to a lengthy chat.

'Have you heard from Francine since she went back to Paris?' he asked. 'She must be at your brother's hotel by now?'

Albert slurped his coffee, smacked his lips as he set the cup down. 'We had a note telling us she'd arrived safely. She'll be settled in by now; quite determined, she was, to have a proper go at the job this time round.'

'She can manage it, if anyone can! You must be missing her, though?'

'Humph! Lucette wasn't very happy to lose her, but what can you do? Albert gave a twisted smile. 'Always had a mind of her own, that girl.'

She'd only lasted a few weeks working in Lanvier's pharmacy, Marcel knew that much. Rumours were still circulating; not a good idea, getting too friendly with the boss's pride and joy of a son.

Albert was elaborating on the business of the hotel, '. . . so as you can imagine, George keeps her busy. All those German chaps need beds too, when all is said and done. The Hôtel du Poirier is in a prime spot, bang in the middle of Montmartre, you know.'

Marcel set his cup aside, suddenly attentive. 'I heard the Gestapo had quite a big sweep around Paris. Montmartre was one of their targets, wasn't it?'

Albert gave him a wary look, his gaze travelling from the door to the shop window and back again. He leaned in, lowered his voice. 'I've not said anything to Lucette, she'd get herself into a such a state, no good would come of it. George did send word of a raid on the hotel.' He paused for a moment, measuring the impact of his news.

'Crack of dawn, it was, when they started banging on the front door. Would have smashed it in if the receptionist hadn't looked smart, opened up straight away. A Kraut waved a document at him, read a list of garbled names, wouldn't take no for an answer. The Gestapo went through the whole place with a toothcomb, every room.'

'Must have been embarrassing for his guests!'

'To say the least! George told me it didn't take long; once they got what they wanted, they cleared off. Dragged away one of the chamber maids and a caretaker, shoved them into a van and away they went, just like that.'

Marcel gave a low whistle.

'Francine was quite put out; the maid was a friend of hers.'

'Doesn't sound like she'll be seeing her friend for a little while. If ever. But did she manage to find out what happened to her?'

'George gave her permission to go along to the *Vel 'D 'Hiv\**, to see if anything could be done. Couldn't get into the place, barricades everywhere, cordonned off right the way round. A few days later, she goes back and finds the place deserted.'

'They were probably sent on to one of those transit camps: Tourelles, Drancy, Pithiviers. The Germans will have some scheme or other . . .'

Albert yawned as he stretched his arms out, dropping them into his lap. He began to crack his knuckles. 'Not our problem. Only Jews, after all.'

Marcel drew a deep breath, brimming with indignation. Stopping himself just in time, he said, 'With all this upheaval in Paris, it's no wonder Lucette prefers Francine to stay home.'

Albert grunted affirmation, reaching for his tobacco pouch. He began to roll up, again, speculative looks cast at his friend, as his fingers performed their task. Marcel scratched his ear, his gaze trained on the shop window. The old boy seemed to have something else on his mind, altogether. Typical of him to wait all this time to come out with it. From the depths of the living quarters, a crash of something tumbling, followed by the rise and fall of an admonishing voice. Smoke rings floated around them, dissolving, dispersing. Albert seemed lost in thought. Stirring at last, he shifted in his seat.

'Ay, Marcel, women are contrary, you've got to admit it.'

It was just as though they'd been engaged in a lengthy discussion on the subject. Marcel leaned towards him, assuming an expression of empathetic attention, but Albert seemed to be immersed in his own reflections. He heaved a sigh, cleared his throat, spat on the flagstone floor.

'That daughter of mine, she's a rum one, all right.'

Marcel froze for a moment, then gave a sigh of concurrence. It must be Francine. 'Paris is no place for a young woman these days,' he agreed.

Albert clicked his tongue, shedding fragments of tobacco. 'I wasn't thinking of Francine, not that that girl could do anything to surprise me.'

Marcel tightened his grip on his thighs, slid them into his trouser pockets.

'It's the other one I'm talking about. Just when I was beginning to . . . ' he cast an aggrieved glance at Marcel.

Marcel could only play for time. 'Such a sweet, even-tempered young lass, I find it hard to believe she'd give you any trouble.'

'Ah, sweet enough to look at, but contrary by nature, that's for sure.' Albert picked up his coffee cup, contemplating the muddy dregs, then waved it at Marcel, as if in accusation.

'I thought you were taking a special interest in that girl? I've seen you about with her often enough.'

Marcel gave an embarrassed laugh. 'Is that all! Lucette asked me if I'd mind going along with Thérèse to the Marivale farm a couple of times, just to make sure she was going to be safe.' There was certainly enough truth in his account to keep his old friend happy. 'I thought you would have known,' he added, hoping to reinforce his point.

Albert gave a puzzled frown, scratching his head. Evidently this was a subject Lucette hadn't discussed with him.

'I must admit,' Marcel continued, with a wry smile, 'your daughter was not exactly keen to have my company.' He could still see the anxious, furtive glances, the down-turned head. 'She's a good girl, though, knows well enough not to argue with her mother.'

On reflection, he had to admit that he might have been just a little carried away that last time. Lucette had already told him that Thérèse could easily manage the journey on her own, thank you very much. It just so happened that on his way home one evening, there she was, trotting down the lane, dangling that little *pot au lait* of hers. He'd downed a couple of beers at Odette's, perhaps even a few more. The upshot of it was, that he ended up making himself a bit of a nuisance, tagging along, trying to coax a few words out of her. That coy shyness seemed like a clear invitation; irresistible. He should have remembered she wasn't much more than a child.

His tone became admonishing. 'It's not a good idea these days, as you know, letting a pretty girl go around unchaperoned, especially if it's late in the day. You never can be quite sure you'll be safe with the Boche roaming around. Off duty, anything could happen.'

31

When he kissed her, she let out a shriek, then whisked herself off, scampering like a rabbit. He'd been wondering ever since whether she'd gone mewling to Papa. Kept clear of the workshop for about a month to let things settle down. Evidently it still wasn't long enough. What a fool he'd been!

Albert was on his feet, restless. He wandered over to the workbench and began to fidget with his cutting tools, picking them up at random, setting them down again. 'I've heard of a few incidents, you don't need to elaborate. Even so . . .'

This was the right moment to focus on his brother. 'Let's get the story straight, then you'll know what's what. As you know, Laurence came back home after his last race at Longchamp, he wasn't exactly the picture of health. After a few days in bed he was up again, kicking his heels, hanging about, not knowing what to do with himself. So I put it to him, "why don't you offer your services as an escort for Thérèse? Make yourself useful, at least, until you're well enough to get some proper work." As it happens, the very next week I had to go over to Argentan. Cornu wanted me to do a stint at his other sawmill, they were short of manpower.' It was quite convenient, the way it turned out; Lucette didn't mind the new arrangement and it obviously suited Thérèse.

Albert seemed only partly mollified. 'But now she's on and on about that brother of yours: it's Laurence this and Laurence that, till the cows come home. Then when he does appear she clams up, goes all starry eyed.' He shook his head with a foreboding air.

'Wasting her time, that's what I think.'

Marcel gave a dismissive smile, trying not to show his relief. He certainly owed his brother a drink. 'Nothing to get so worked up about, Albert, she's only a child, really. Young girls, they get these obsessions.'

Albert wasn't going to let it go yet. 'All very well for you, giving your brother a chance to shine, but that's no reason to drop out of circulation, just like that, without a word of warning. Pierre told me you didn't stay more than a week on that Argentan job.'

Marcel muttered apologies, at a loss for words. Keeping away from the workshop seemed to have done more harm than good. Albert's gimlet eyes were still trained on him. He cocked his head with a knowing look.

'If you and Laurence are making use of her to play out some sort of sibling wager, I'll have both your hides, that I will. Make a change from the cows!' The gruff humour of his tone had more than a bitter edge to it.

Marcel shifted on the workbench, recalling, with embarassment, the flippant exchange he'd had with Laurence. 'She's all yours,' he'd told him, 'I can't be bothered with an unripe peach when there are plenty of ripe ones to be plucked.' The two of them had parted in perfect accord.

All in the past, best forgotten. On his feet now, he planted himself in front of Albert, shaking his head in genial exasperation.

'Listen! You've got the wrong end of the stick, Albert, we're not the sort of lads to treat a daughter of yours like that!'

Albert gave a doubtful haruumph as he rummaged through a box under the workbench. With a grunt of satisfaction he pulled out a well-oiled brown paper parcel, unfolding it with care, selecting a pattern to spread out across the hide. Marcel recognised the familiar outline of a saddle. With a sigh of resignation, Albert began to smooth the creases out.'Ah, well, can't be helped, I suppose. Got my hopes up for a while, thinking you'd be on the way to becoming a son-in-law, you know.' .

'It would be more than I deserve,' Marcel replied, lowering his head. He would try to make amends, he told himself.

Albert was elaborating on his views of Laurence '. . . bit of a charmer, though, isn't he, I suppose that's what she's fallen for.'

'Runs in the blood,' Marcel agreed.

There was a snort of appreciation, but Albert was soon shaking his head with a brooding look. He waved a ruler at Marcel. 'She might go weak at the knees for him but it'll all end in trouble, you mark my words.'

Marcel felt he could afford to defend his brother, now. 'We needn't be so sure of that. He's got a good heart and a caring disposition, that's what really counts.'

Albert picked up a cutting knife and ran his finger along the edge to test the blade. 'Can't see that boy settling down with a wife for a long time yet.' He bent over his task.

'He'll find his feet, just you wait and see,' Marcel responded. 'Who would have thought that he'd be taken on at the stables of Duke Du Plessis, then selected to be trained up as a jockey?'

'Fat lot of use that is now he's been laid off,' Albert retorted. 'Besides, there's not many can afford that sort of livery turnout, the way things are going these days.' He turned round to confront Marcel, waving his knife at him.

'What kind of prospects has he got, I ask you! With his history of health problems, how is he ever going to get a proper job again? Even if there wasn't a war on, I can't see there'd be much chance of anything for that lad!'

'I shouldn't worry, Albert. Laurence and Thérèse, they're a pair of youngsters, really, I wonder if they've even given the future a thought?' Marcel's voice took on a cajoling tone. 'Surely, you can remember what it was like at that age, can't you?' By all accounts, Albert's marriage had been hastily arranged.

'Hmph! Things were different in those day,' Albert replied, turning his attention to the task in hand. He began to cut into the hide, guiding the knife around the pattern. As if by mutual consent, conversation reverted to a casual exchange of local news and gossip.

The door of the workshop door grated, setting the bell jangling in refrain. Laurence pushed his way through. There was a moment's hesitation in his gait while he smothered a cough, evidently registering the intensity of the fumes, before he decided to make the best of it.

'Could have sworn I'd just wandered into the Duke's stables. You make me feel right at home.' Albert glanced up at him, his eyes narrowing in a look of measured appraisal.

'I laid it on especially for you, of course. Go on through, young man, get yourself a cup of coffee, that's what you're here for, isn't it? The women will sort you out.'

Laurence darted an enquiring look at Marcel. A nod and a wink from him was reassurance enough.

'Thanks, Monsieur Griot! I'll see you later.' He hurried towards the connecting door, whistling under his breath.

# Confession

She was calling out from the top of the stairs. 'Have you seen my prayer book, Maman? I've searched everywhere!' Lucette gave a sigh. Sometimes she felt she could hardly cope with so much devotion in that child of hers. 'You'll come to confession with me this time?' Thérèse had asked, soft eyes entreating. Impossible to refuse.

'Have a look under the pillows,' Lucette called up to her, 'or it could be under Nicolas's bed. I'll check down here.'

The boy was very likely to have hidden it in some unlikely place out of sheer mischief, she knew well enough. Her sewing basket was a favoured, though forbidden cache. She rifled through the heap of socks spilling out of it; when was she ever going to find time to darn them? No sign of it here. Perhaps he'd buried it in the sack of laundry Heinrich had brought round earlier? Nicolas had been first at the door, she remembered, lingering, enthralled, while Heinrich exchanged a few words with her.

Upending the sack, she gave it a vigorous shake. Mostly grey shirts this time. She must remember to give them a good soak in the cauldron. It made a useful bit of income, taking in washing, but some of those German soldiers were so fussy, it wasn't worth taking any short cuts. No prayer book here. Nicolas would confess, however reluctantly, but where was he?

She stepped into the garden to scan the terrain. Some of the hens started towards her, clucking, as she waved them off. Minou brushed against her legs, ever hopeful.

The workshop was the first place she should have thought of. Albert was at his bench by the window, stitching a harness. Nicolas crouched over a heap of leather off-cuts in the corner, absorbed in his latest project.

'Look Maman, I'm making a lasso,' he announced, brandishing a straggling length of roughly fastened scraps. 'It's going to be just like Cowboy Mickey. Felix showed me the comic but he wouldn't let me take it home, not even for one night!'

'What a clever boy. Now tell me, what have you done with . .'

'He's so mean! Anyway, I can still remember how it goes, I'll show him!'

Thérèse's voice rang out: 'Found it, Maman!' One problem disposed of, at least.

'I'm sure you'll be able to make a very good one, Nicolas. Now listen. I've got to go to church with Thérèse for a little while. You'll stay here with Papa, won't you?'

Nicolas didn't even look up. 'Course I'm staying here! I want to finish my lasso so I can show Felix tomorrow. He's going to want one too, you wait and see.'

Albert was stitching a harness. He glanced up, tarred thread in hand, as she touched his shoulder.

'Perhaps you could remind Nicolas about feeding the rabbits, Albert, if you don't mind? There's a basin of vegetable trimmings by the kitchen door.'

He let out an affirmative grunt, intent on his work. 'Don't be long, I've promised to meet Daniel Richaud and Pierre at Odette's later on.'

Thérèse was outside the door, shifting impatiently from one foot to the other. Lucette linked arms with her as they set off for the church. Late afternoon sun bathed the high street in a mellow glow, highlighting creamy ripples of lace curtains in windows. Clusters of ghostly flowers bloomed, frosted white leaves clustering in mesh nets. Geraniums flared against a shaded wall. No time to linger, she reminded herself. Father Benoît would be in the confessional, but only until five o'clock. Thérèse was urging her on.

They waved at Adèle on the steps of the café, shaking out a tablecloth. Nearly two years now since that first encounter in the *lavoir*. How fortunate that Odette had decided to take mother and child under her wing; she was more than willing to provide a spare room in exchange for help in the café and shop. Having a little one about took her mind off her own losses. War had taken her husband, diphtheria her child.

Outside Oléron Printers, a man was unloading boxes from a cart, whistling cheerfully. Marcel Richaud, again. He was lucky to be taken on, Albert had told her. No experience to offer; if it hadn't been for Doctor Menier, he wouldn't have stood a chance.

Marcel whisked his cap off, offering a pantomime bow. 'What a pleasure it is to see such fine ladies taking a stroll at the end of a working day.'

Lucette laughed politely, giving her daughter's arm a reassuring squeeze. She had no objection to Marcel's good-natured antics, but Thérèse kept her head down, shifting her feet.

To cover her daughter's embarrassment, Lucette hastened to congratulate Marcel on his new position. The affirmative reply was more than cheerful. 'Hard graft, of course, being an apprentice, but I'm learning something new every day.'

'That's good. Quite taken by surprise, we were, when we first heard about it. Your mother told me that working at the sawmill has always been a family tradition.'

Marcel snorted. 'Is that what she said? Time for a change, then, I should think; they can manage well enough without me. Cornu has taken on a couple of Belgians desperate for work. Cheaper to run as far as he's concerned and a good enough excuse for me to move on.'

He gestured towards the open door of the printing workshop. 'Nice secure little setup this is too, a lot more scope to it. Almanacs, of course, they've built up their reputation on them. But also, you wouldn't believe the number of religious tracts they churn out here. Quite a demand for them, these days, it's a job to find enough paper. Every new edition gets trimmed down a bit. . . '

Thérèse gave her an agitated nudge. 'Maman, we'll be late if we don't hurry.'

Marcel was all apology, sweeping his arm wide to encourage their passage. 'So sorry, *mesdames*, I had no idea you were on your way to an appointment. I wouldn't dream of detaining you a moment longer.'

'Give my best regards to your mother,' Lucette called out, smiling over her shoulder. Thérèse bowed her head, steering her mother onwards.

The heavy padded door of the church swished behind them. They hurried down the nave, heels clicking. The tiled floor reflected a muted kaleidoscope of reds, greens, blues, from stained glass windows set high in the walls. They passed the statue of St. James, glowing behind a rack of candles, genuflected before the altar and turned into the transept.

The confessional leaned against the wall of a side chapel, a sombre, forbidding presence. Lucette peered at the gap under the curtain to catch the glint of polished black shoes. Father Benoît was waiting.

'You first, my dear,' she whispered to her daughter. 'I need to collect my thoughts.' Thérèse pressed her hand, gratefully, and was gone.

It was a relief to sink into a pew, let herself rest for a few minutes. Constant fatigue was one of the symptoms, she remembered it well. She eased the belt at her waist, feeling for another eyelet. Three months now. After a gap of nearly eight years, so unexpected. That last miscarriage, she'd taken it as a sign that she couldn't have any more. How wrong she'd been.

Thérèse would be shocked, Francine, contemptuous. She gave a wry smile. Albert, of course, hadn't even noticed. He'd said to her, once, that he wouldn't mind having another boy about the house, but that was a long time ago, before the Germans came, before the war started. What would he think, now?

The sound of light footsteps startled her, she must have drifted off. Thérèse was smiling, her face a soft radiance. Luctte eased herself into motion as her daughter sank to her knees.

Approaching the confessional, her feet dragged, lead weights sinking. She found herself longing to go straight past, down the nave, through the door, into the street. But where would she go? What could she do? Father Benoît was waiting. Thérèse needed her. This was the life she had. This was what was expected of her.

Lifting the coarse black curtain of the confessional, she stepped into enveloping darkness and settled onto the well-worn *prie-dieu**. Wooden panels hemmed her in, close as a coffin. Lingering traces of lavender water tempered the pervading odour of perspiration and stale scent. She heard Father Benoît shift in his dark cubbyhole. He cleared his throat, the signal for her to begin.

'In the name of the Father and of the Son and of the Holy Spirit. My last confession was. . .' How long ago? She sifted through her recent past, helplessly. It must have been before she knew. . . In a low voice, she continued. 'My last confession was three months ago.'

A weary sigh of resignation fanned her forehead. 'Carry on, my child.'

She ran through the habitual litany of sins cropping up during the routine of daily life: the frustration, as she failed to order her household, giving rise to impatience and anger. Nicolas had provoked her rare but most enduring outbursts.

Father Benoît chided her gently, exhorting her to repeat the Prayer of Contrition when she came to the end of her account.

'Almighty God. I am heartily sorry for having offended you and I . . .' Her voice caught in a rising tide of emotion.

Her confessor spoke with renewed concern. 'Was there anything else, my child?' Darkness wrapped itself round, submerging her. Sounding through the depths came the insistent voice: 'If you are aware of any other sins, it is your Christian duty to confess them.'

She knew what she needed to say now, nothing else really mattered. But how could she begin. Taking a fractured breath, she forced the preliminary words out.

'Father, I am with child again.'

She could feel the relief in his sigh. 'Congratulations, my child. You have been blessed.'

How could she explain? 'Thank you, Father. Every child is a blessing, I know, but now, after all this time . . . I find myself resenting God's gift to me.'

The silence was palpable, a throbbing pulse. Having confessed so much, she clutched at whatever pitiful excuses she could muster up.

'I am weak and tired, Father; I hardly know how to bear it.'

His voice cut into her anguish like cold tempered steel. 'Is the child lawfully conceived in the sanctity of holy wedlock?'

She sat back on her heels. It hadn't occurred to her that anyone could think otherwise.

'Oh yes, of course, Father,' she stammered, 'of course. That's not the problem. It's just that . . .'

How could she explain? What could she say? That Nicolas wore her down, that she barely had time to turn round. That they were hard pressed, even now, to make ends meet. Her head sank into her hands. How could she confess that the problem was really so much more, that Albert had become the cross she had to bear, the shared bed her punishment. God would strike her dead, no doubt, but this child was not welcome. Tears bathed her palms. She tried to suppress the sobs rising from the depths of her chest.

Father Benoît spoke with anxious concern, now. 'Calm yourself, daughter in Christ, be calm, now. Let the weight of your sins be taken from you.' The compassionate tones released a torrent of long repressed feelings. Words came pouring out.

'It's all a mistake, Father, I never should have let him . . .I was so young, so naïve, I didn't know what I was doing . . .'

That mid-summer evening when everything changed came flooding back. The nervous excitement of a young girl peering into a tarnished mirror, trying to see herself through his eyes. That anxious half-hour of eternity thinking she'd never be able to escape from the house without being noticed. Then the mad rush down the lane, willow whipping her face in passing, a fallen branch rising to meet her, to arrive at last, flushed, breathless, suddenly bashful. He stood there, without saying a word, regarding her with what she hoped would be amused approval. A surge of elation coursed through her body, a sudden realisation that she could be attractive to a man, even this older man whom she found so intriguing. He took her hand, stroking it like fur on a cat's back, gave a chuckle when she pulled away. He made her laugh with stories of his brothers and the tricks they played on each other. She felt carefree, exhilarated.

They were on their way home when he took her arm, leaning into her to point out the owl he'd spotted on the oak tree just ahead, teasing her when she couldn't see it, then drawing closer, gently easing her chin round. She drew tight fists to her cheeks at the memory of his face melting into hers, an urgent mouth prising her lips apart, tongue crawling round the inside of her mouth. He pulled her up against him, kneading his hands into her skin, fingers urgently seeking secret places she was ashamed to seem to notice, even now, afraid to protest about. She closed her eyes, shook her head. What a fool she'd been.

'I gave him what he seemed to expect and need, Father,' she said at last, 'that's the terrible truth. But it wasn't what everyone else expected.' Her cheek remembered the sting of her mother's fierce slap, the day her condition could no longer be concealed. She could never forget the tirade of withering contempt from her father, before he stomped out the door to track down 'that miserable cur.' The result, a hastily arranged marriage, by special licence, in her uncle's parish: no friends and neighbours invited to witness her shame.

She pulled herself up, straightened her back, sniffing into her handkerchief. 'All these years, Father, I've tried to make the best of my marriage, to be a dutiful wife to my husband, a good mother to the children.' She squeezed her handkerchief into a ball. 'Now it's as though God has told me, no, this isn't enough, what you've done, this isn't enough to redeem your sin; I'm going to make you start all over again. It doesn't seem fair. . .' She buried her face in her hands. 'I'm sorry Father, I never meant to come out with such words, I hardly know what I'm saying. . .'

There was a long silence, brought to an end with a sigh. 'I understand, my dear. Try to compose yourself. You won't be the only woman to express resentment concerning a forthcoming birth. That is without even taking into consideration the pregnancies arising out of wedlock, more numerous than you could imagine.' He paused, clearing his throat. 'God's purpose in this cannot always be understood. Indeed, it is part of our task to exercise due humility, to accept that ultimately, his purpose may well remain beyond out understanding.'

He paused, as if waiting for her to take in his words. 'But this is not a sufficient reason to show ingratitude or to challenge His will.' She winced under the severe stroke of admonition, hardly taking in his subsequent, more positive assertions. 'Goodness will come of it,' he was saying now, 'of that I have no doubt.'

She lifted her head from her hands. If she could believe his words, everything would be so simple.

'I am asking you to shed your resentment and fear,' he was saying, 'to bear with humility your unwanted gift, so that you may learn to accept your condition with grace and due thanks. Your body may be weak: we are all mortal creatures after all, subject to these frailties, but this God given trial will make you stronger in spirit.'

The silence echoed with the resonance of his words. 'Now go,' he continued, his tone emphatic, 'reflect on your condition, pray that you may one day be giving thanks for it. You must turn to Our Lady for her blessing and protection. Remember to say a special prayer to Her every single day of this week.' She heard the chair creaking as he shifted his weight. 'And now, let us bring your confession to an end. Give thanks to the Lord for He is good.'

'For His mercy endureth forever,' she responded, dutifully, making the sign of the cross.

Thérèse was still rapt in her devotions. Lucette knelt some distance away and drew her rosary from her bag, letting the beads run through her fingers. Father Benoît had responded with more understanding than she'd expected. She smiled, quietly, marvelling at the old priest. After all these years, he still knew how to get through to her. An image of her sixteen year old self came to mind: the frightened girl cowering in the church porch just before the wedding, Father Benoît calming her with a light touch and a few kind words.

'Don't worry, Mademoiselle Badin,' he'd said, 'we're all in God's hands.'

She slipped the rosary into her bag, beckoned to Thérèse. God willing, she would manage it, the girls would help. Albert might even be pleased.

The sun was just setting behind the row of shops as they made their way back along the street. Adèle waved as they passed the café, calling out a greeting. Thérèse asked after Sonia, made a fuss of the child when she appeared.

They found Nicolas with Xavier in front of the house, kicking a soggy football back and forth, oblivious of their presence. Before long, Clémence would be calling for Xavier, in the meantime, they could prepare supper, summoning Nicholas when it was ready. He'd pay no attention, of course, probably ignore a second summons as well. Albert would take over, threatening dire punishment. Nicolas would sidle in, dragging his heels. Lucette smiled, in spite of herself, at the predictable rhythm of family life.

# Peeling

Peeling potatoes in the scullery that evening, she caught the sound of his voice coming from the workshop, that low, smooth cadence she knew so well. Her hands gripped the knife, trembling. A coil of mottled brown peel hung suspended, spinning, quivering gently, before it tumbled, plop, into the basin of cream white mounds. She set the knife down, lifted a corner of the apron to wipe her hands, every sense alert to the ebb and flow of conversation.

At least two weeks now since her evening walks came to an abrupt termination. 'No more cream from the farm,' Maman had announced one day, 'Madame Marivale wants too many coupons. You'd think there'd be a concession for her loyal friends and neighbours,' she went on, sputtering with indignation. 'We can do without from now on, see how she likes that!' Thérèse kept silent, not wanting to give herself away. No more opportunities for those prolonged walks, for casual meetings which had become almost a routine. Two weeks was surely time enough to forget him, but look how her pulse was racing now, the heat rising to her cheeks.

She listened to the interminable exchanges bouncing back and forth, relieved to hear laughter easing into parting expressions of good will. He and Papa were getting on only too well these days. The door slammed shut. Footsteps in the passage echoed in her chest. She peered at her reflection in the gleaming lid of a saucepan, agitated fingers patting her hair into place.

When Laurence came through she was intent on potatoes again, a serious occupation. He stopped short, boots jangling, one hand resting on his hip, as he surveyed her. She couldn't help stealing a look, meeting his gaze for a long moment, a tremor of a smile edging round her lips, before casting her eyes down. Milky water rippled in the basin as her hands dipped in and out.

'*Bonsoir, Mademoiselle. . .*' Laurence was smiling as he strolled towards the kitchen range. 'I don't suppose there'd be a cup of coffee for a hard-working jockey, would there?'

She reached for the coffee pot, trying not to let him see how pleased she was.

# JUNE – NOVEMBER 1943

# The Game

He was quenching his thirst with a bock* at Odette's when a weathered hand slid across the table. André was looming over him, smiling, blandly. 'Fancy a game of *palet*?'* he asked.

'Come again?' Marcel could barely conceal his surprise. André stood firm, waiting for the message to sink in. Marcel prevaricated, giving way after a convincing display of reluctance. You never knew who might be within earshot.

'Sunday afternoon, five o'clock, in the park?' It wasn't really a question. André was already hastening towards the door, waving to his friends in parting.

Perfect cover for a meeting, Marcel reflected, Menier knew what he was about. A friendly game of *palet sur planche*, who could quibble about that?

The weather was on their side that Sunday, plenty of warm sun, though a fresh breeze from the west kept the temperature down. The church clock chimed the hour just as he passed the stone lintels of the park entrance. At the far end of the games pitch, André and Menier were struggling to shift the *planche** on the coarse sand.

'Give us a hand, would you?' Menier called out. 'We can't seem to get it level.' They stabilised the board at last, stamping, to firm it down, just as Robert and Henri strolled over. Robert and Henri to him, of course, he knew that they had been given pseudonyms. 'For the security of our cell group, you've got to live and breathe with an alias identity,' Menier had told them. 'I don't want the wrong names to slip out if you are unfortunate enough to be detained.' Lucien, he reminded himself, again, that's who I am now.

Menier was greeting the new arrivals with welcoming handshakes and friendly exchanges, organising the match as though this was their only concern.

'Heads or tails?' he demanded, tossing a coin as they drew round. 'Right. André, Lucien, you're on.' After this outburst of efficiency, Menier seemed to relax. Delving into his pocket, he pulled out a red target disc and started tossing it from one hand to the other. 'After the message I picked up from the *pianiste*,* he said, 'I was going to cancel this meeting altogether.' His eyes darted round the assembled group. Henri was the only one who looked puzzled.

'Then I reconsidered, decided it would be best to carry on as though it meant nothing to us. Just a bit of a friendly match between friends. . .'

'This message you've picked up,' Henri interrupted, 'you'll need to spell it out for me. Whatever it is, I certainly haven't been told.'

Menier was ready for him. 'I shouldn't worry about that, Henri. There's been a lot of confusion about what happened, we're only beginning to get it straight.' He lowered his voice. 'Some of you will have heard that René Hardy[3] has just been arrested. We've had a message from Pineau, telling us to put our latest operation on hold for the moment. The Boche are certain to be cracking down, taking a hard line. More vigilance, for a start, reprisals are anticipated. We've got to let things cool down a bit, clarify the situation before we activate our plans.'

A couple of German soldiers sauntered through the gates of the park. On the alert, Menier brandished the target disc. 'Here you are, André! Catch! Look sharp, now. Try to land it somewhere on the board!' Easy to laugh at that one, André was probably the best player there.

As the game got under way, the soldiers drew nearer, evidently curious to see what kind of bizarre activities French civilians got up to. Menier greeted them affably, making the most of his self-appointed role as the genial doctor having an afternoon off. He launched into a detailed explanation of the game, airing his fluent German as and when it suited him.

'. . . a Breton game, yes, from Brittany, *Britanien*, that's a remote region over that way,' he waved towards the West. 'The game caught on, travelled into Lower Normandy.' His hands dipped and spread out. 'We've been having games here since I was a child. *Wenn Ich ein Kind war.*' Pointing at the square wooden game board, he said, 'There you can see the *planche*, a traditional one made of poplar. There are two teams, *Zwei Manschaften*.' Two fingers were raised, for good measure. 'Each player is supposed to have two or as many as four *palets*. They're made of iron, *Eisen*. Yes, *Eisen*, he repeated. 'You see the red one over there? That's the *maître*, the target. *Ziel*,' he shouted, relishing their perplexed expressions. 'Now, the purpose of the game is to score points by hitting the target, or at least landing as close to it as you can. Each player takes turns throwing, like so,' here he mimed the action impeccably, 'and then they add up the score. The first team to get twelve points, *zwoelf punkten*, wins the game. *Gewinns das Spiel*. Each match consists of. . .'

'He's making every effort to bore the socks off them so they'll move on, Marcel murmured to André.

'It's working,' André chuckled, leaning over to check the position of the disc he'd just thrown. 'Look how they're shuffling their feet. One of them is stealing a glance at his watch.'

'There they go,' Marcel confirmed. 'Look how Menier tags alongside, still holding forth, giving them full measure. They're completely baffled, what a hoot.'

The doctor was back with them soon enough, rubbing his hands in satisfaction. 'They won't bother us again for a while.' He surveyed the progress of the game. 'On we go. Your turn, Lucien, isn't it? He prodded Marcel, a sharp reminder of his cell group name. 'You can take your turn while I'm having a word with the others. ' He gestured to gather the rest of the group around him.

'As I was saying, before our little interruption, there's one project on hold, now, but that doesn't mean we're going to remain idle. The RAF will be dropping the next batch of leaflets soon, probably a schedule for the forthcoming broadcasts. We need to be on hand for distribution, I'm just waiting for a date and a time.'

'Nice one, Lucien,' he called out, watching a disc impact with a thud on top of another one. 'Our first *chapeau*.'*

'A total fluke,' Marcel responded, shaking out his pitching hand in disbelief. Menier had already turned back towards the others. 'André, Robert, are you up for collection duties? It's very likely that you'll need to be ready at short notice.'

Marcel listened to the negotiations carried out during the next few rounds of play, wondering why Menier hadn't asked him to take on the job. Now that he had become an apprentice type-setter, he felt a proprietorial interest in anything to do with leaflet publication and distribution.

A break in the discussion came at last. 'If you need someone else, Menier, I'll be very happy to oblige.'

'Can't spare you,' Menier replied, shortly, scratching marks in the sand to tally up the score. You're on next, Robert.' Marcel was turning away, shoulders stiff, when he felt a restraining hand on his arm. 'I'm holding you in reserve for another project, if you're willing. Tell you in a moment.'

A group of children raced towards them, squealing with excitement. Marcel sighed. Nicolas, again, the lad had a talent for pitching up when he wasn't welcome. His two urchin friends must be Pierre's children, no mistaking those ginger heads. And wasn't that little Sonia trailing behind them, sucking her thumb? The children were buzzing round

Menier, pelting him with questions, angling for sweets. Persuaded to occupy a nearby bench, they squirmed and kicked, giggling, as they nudged each other. After a heated exchange of whispers, Nicolas peeled away from his friends to sidle up to Marcel.

'Can I have a go,' he begged. I'm a good shot, I'll show you how . . .'

'What about me, I'm much better than you are,' the smallest boy bragged, jumping down from the bench to elbow Nicolas aside.

Marcel sighed, sank to his haunches, a better position to level with the boys. 'We're playing a match, now,' he explained, 'can't interrupt it for everyone who wants to play, otherwise we'd never finish. You see what I mean, don't you?' A whimpering chorus of protests started up. 'Now, listen, what if you organise another sort of game?' He suddenly noticed that every child was staring, in various degrees of consternation, at the distant figure of a woman approaching at full speed.

'Aha, there you are!' That hoarse voice, unmistakeable, though he couldn't even remember the last time their paths had crossed. Francine had caught up with them now, grim displeasure marring the striking features he had often admired. He took note of the full, sensuous lips, high cheek bones, the rather long, masculine nose. Her dark hair was swept back, evidently without regard, into a loose chignon. A voluminous apron covered what seemed to be a rather skimpy dress; the whole ensemble doing little justice to a magnificent form. What a power house, he told himself, sucking in his breath. He strode towards her, extending his hand.

'Good evening, Francine, what a pleasure to see you in town again.'

'Ah, Monsieur Richaud, it's been a long time.' A polite, distracted smile flickered across her face. 'Please excuse me, but those children . . .'

Nicolas was skulking behind the other children. She pushed them aside to pounce on the lad, shaking him by the shoulders. 'I told you not to go running off to the park, didn't I? So then what happens? I turn my back for one minute and you're gone, you cheeky little . . .'

'I didn't go to the park,' Nicolas whined, 'I didn't mean to go, I went to Xavier's house and he wanted me to go with him. . .' Sonia regarded their exchange, eyes wide with alarm. Now she burst into tears.

Albert had been looking forward to Francine's return, Marcel remembered. 'A firm hand, that's what we need. We're all at sixes and sevens with the new babe in the house. My daughter will know what to do.' From the looks of it, she'd taken on household management in full measure. He stood back, catching Francine's eye, offering a nod and a smile as she marched off with her little troop.

Menier couldn't resist a military salute. 'I like a girl with spirit,' he said, watching her stride along, dragging little Sonia by one arm, 'she does get a bit carried away, though.' He gave a chuckle. 'Those children will be only too pleased when she decides to go back to Paris again.'

Marcel was standing apart from the others, watching the final round of the match, when Menier appeared by his side. 'How are you getting on at the printers?' he asked.

Well aware that Menier was the one who'd secured the position for him, Marcel launched into a glowing report, glossing over the more negative aspects of the job: the endless clearing up they left for him, the extra hours at short notice, the fiery temper of Monsieur Dambert.

'Are you on your own there, from time to time?'

'Well yes, quite often, I suppose.' He began to realise what Menier was leading up to.

Menier nodded. 'Good. I'm going to ask you whether, under appropriate circumstances, you might be able to find time to run off some news sheets for us?'

'You mean, something on the lines of '*La Voix du Nord*[4]?' That's quite an undertaking,' Marcel responded, a note of caution edging his voice.

'Oh, nothing that elaborate, more of a supplement is what I had in mind.'

Cheers and enthusiastic clapping brought their attention back to the game in progress. Robert had nearly hit the target.

'Well done, Robert!' Menier called out, giving him a thumbs up. He turned back to Marcel.

'Let me explain my little scheme. As you know, in our dealings with the Huns, there are certain problems we come up against all the time. The *relève** for example. The Boche have been cracking down, lately, conscripting men from the age of eighteen, packing them onto trains taking them to Germany, where they work like slaves in the munitions factories.'

'Don't I know it!' Marcel rejoined. The pit of his stomach hollowed out as he contemplated his inevitable fate. His move from Potigny to Marigny might have thrown a spoke in the works, but it was only a temporary reprieve. The STO demand for his services could arrive any day now.

'These men are threatened and intimidated,' Menier continued, 'frightened into obedience. Off they go, rather than face the consequences. We want to encourage them to resist conscription. By

49

spelling out some of the options they can take to avoid obligatory service, we can show them how to resist and still be able to survive to tell the tale.'

'I'm with you, all the way,' Marcel replied, feelingly.

'We could start with a small print run of a hundred leaflets,' Menier continued, 'make it clear that resistance is not so impossible, once you know the options. Doctors' certificates, muddled paperwork, false identities, all sorts of devices.'

Marcel weighed up his chances. Monsieur Dambert never stayed on late if he could help it. The others had families to get back to. There should be time enough for a small print run after hours. He found himself nodding agreement.

'I'll let you know next time an evening shift comes up, should be able to manage something then.'

The bell in the church tower rang out: five, six, seven o'clock already. 'You must be absolutely certain that you're not going to be interrupted,' Menier warned him. 'You'd lose more than your job if you got shopped, you know that.'

'I won't take any chances.'

André was scoring off points with a stick, Henri's voice a few decibels higher with each number he called out. 'Thirty-one, thirty-two, Thirty-three, forty-three. *Merde!* We've lost! And here was I thinking they'd never catch up.'

'It's that *chapeau* made all the difference,' Robert pronounced. He thrust out a hand. 'André, Lucien, congratulations.'

'Hang this curfew,' Marcel expostulated, 'this would have been the perfect excuse for a little celebrations at Odette's!'

'We'll put it on hold until we've managed to kick the Huns out of town,' Menier promised.

At the entrance to the park, the ritual leave-taking began: handshakes, parting comments, casual expressions of goodwill before they went their separate ways home. Marcel turned into the Grande Rue, deserted except for a large, stationary Mercedes. Menier was speaking very slowly, at top volume, to the person inside.

'It's more likely to be gout, *Herr Kommandant Kroger*. You need to make an effort to reduce your consumption of red wine; no alternative, I'm afraid. And stop eating so much beef, yes, all those lovely *bifteck*, that's what I mean.' There were sounds of protest emerging from the interior of the Mercedes, ignored by the doctor.

'I'm going to prescribe a special dose of Bromide, to be taken three times a day. I'll send some round to you this evening. Keep on soaking your feet in hot salt water, too, as hot as you can bear it, morning and evening.' He straightened up, giving a military salute before backing away from the vehicle.

'*Auf Wiedersehen, Herr Commandant.*'

# Dance

Soft blue chenille cascaded over her head, sliding down to her calves, slipping off one shoulder. Thérèse peered into the blotched mirror in the wardrobe. She shook her head, frowning. Her friend Jeanine would give her that certain look of constrained disapproval. Is that the best you can do, she'd be thinking.

Lucette was pulling and pinching the folds, determined to resolve the problem. 'I could stitch a seam under each arm and take a few tucks in the sleeves,' she proposed, hopefully.

'It's no use, Maman, let's face it. I look like a twelve year old dressed up in her mother's clothes, there's no getting round it.' The dress slithered to the floor, pooling round her ankles. She stepped out, swooped down to gather the folds. Her mother was standing still, a pensive look on her face. Lucette threw her arms around her. Chenille billowed out like a sail.

'Oops! You'll be smothering us, next,' Lucette exclaimed, laughing, in spite of herself.

Thérèse retrieved the garment and draped it over her mother's outstretched arms. 'It doesn't matter, Maman. You know I'll be fine in the old green one, really; it's a lovely soft cotton, and the V-neck suits me, everyone says so. '

'But it's practically threadbare, I don't see why…'

'It's only a dance, Maman, not a reception for the Duke de Sassy!' Laurence wasn't going to be there; she couldn't see much point in trying to make an impact. He'd broken the news to her when they met last week: potential work at some stables near Sées, if he could sort it out with the manager.

'I don't like to let you down, my love,' he said, stroking her cheek, 'but it's unlikely that I'll be able to get back on time.' She gave a secretive smile, remembering the subsequent exchanges.

Maman was still fussing. 'If we just. . . '

'Oh but you've done such a wonderful job patching up the green one it would be a shame not to get some use out of it.' With timely inspiration, she added, 'Perhaps you could lend me your silky looking pink scarf, that would cheer it up. And don't forget, I've got the mother-of-pearl brooch Aunt Mathilde gave me.'

'Blue is such a lovely colour on you,' Lucette murmured.

Thérèse was already half-buried in the wardrobe, rifling through the

52

garments. The smell of moth balls began to permeate the bedroom.
'I hope Nicolas hasn't been sneaking in here again. Ah, here it is, must have slipped off the hanger.'

Lucette was on her knees, folding up the rejected garment with assiduous care. Smoothing out the creases, she tucked the sleeves under to form a neat package. Thérèse watched the proceedings, her face a study in conjecture.

'Why don't you come along too, Maman? You used to love dancing, I remember you told me. It would be such fun, wouldn't it?' She slid to her knees, winding her arm round her mother's waist, nuzzling into her neck. 'Listen to me, Maman! Come with us, you'd love it, I know you would.'

Lucette shook her off with a smile of tolerance. 'Don't be absurd, *ma chérie*, of course I can't do such a thing. A married woman going to a dance! In any case, I can't leave Nicolas and Claude. Albert wouldn't want to be left in charge, you know what he's like.'

Thérèse watched her putting the folded dress away. Clearly, it wasn't going to be easy to persuade her. Poor Maman! She never gave herself time off to recover after Claude was born, always so busy. Surely it would do her good to get out for a few hours?

'But Maman,' she started up again, 'anyone can go, don't you understand? Your friend Odette was there last week. And I'm sure you could ask Aunt Mathilde to come in to look after Claude and Nicolas, just for the evening, she's always telling us she'd like to help. Or there's Germaine Richaud, she wouldn't mind.' Lucette was rummaging through a drawer. 'I could have sworn that scarf was in here.'

'You should have seen your friend Odette, Maman, she can dance the 'Java' better than any of us.'

Lucette shot a disapproving glance at her. 'Thérèse, don't even think of it! Odette hasn't got children. Besides, she runs a café, it's different for her.' Her voice carried an incisive edge.

'Jeanine says she's seen Clémence there, too, her husband doesn't mind a bit.' Thérèse was on her feet now, playing for advantage. She tossed her head, impatiently. 'No one cares about that sort of thing these days, Maman, that's what Adèle tells me. It's so old-fashioned.'

'Here it is,' announced Lucette, brandishing the scarf like a trophy. 'Come, why don't you slip that dress on, we'll see whether it will do. And let's have no more of this nonsense about me going dancing, if you please.'

'All right, Maman,' Thérèse sighed, in reluctant compliance.

Laurence would be coming round on Sunday, she reminded herself, patiently waiting while her mother fumbled with the hooks at her back. He'd attend to Maman, charm her, just like last time, perhaps that would be enough. Taking Maman out dancing could become a project for another day. In the meantime, there were more practical arrangements to resolve.'By the way, Maman, Jeanine is calling round for me at six tonight. I'll take the bicycle, if that's all right with you?'

'This one's almost impossible to fasten, it must have seized up somehow,' Lucette remarked, fingers struggling for purchase on the metal loop. 'You're only going to the community centre, you don't need a bicycle for that.'

'Oh, but it's booked, Maman, didn't you know? The wind band is giving a concert tonight, those same German officers who were playing in the square last week. Our dance evening is going to be in Montmerrei this time. It's not a problem, is it, Maman?'

'Turn round now, we'll try the scarf with it.' Lucette was standing aside, absently twisting it round her forefinger. 'I don't like the idea of you going so far after dark, even with Jeanine. Couldn't you ask Laurence to come with you?'

Thérèse managed to suppress her impatience. Gently lifting her mother's hand, she prised the scarf away. 'He can't come this time, Maman, I did tell you.'

Lucette's face fell. She let out a heavy sigh.

Thérèse draped the scarf round the collar of the green dress, trying out various arrangements of folds and knots as she gazed into the mirror. 'I can't let Jeanine go on her own, Maman, she's my best friend!' She cast a knowing look at her mirror twin. Maman would give way, she always did, in the end.

Sounds from the street drew Lucette to the window. Soldiers strolled by, joking and chatting. There seemed to be more Germans about than ever before; they weren't as well mannered and polite as they used to be. New regulations posted up, too: prohibitions, stricter curfews, warnings. People she knew of had been stopped and interrogated. Sometimes taken away.

One of the soldiers spotted Lucette and gave his companion a nudge. She stepped out of sight and spun round, her face red with indignation. 'If you really insist on attending this dance, Thérèse, I'm going to escort both of you on foot. I'll ask your Papa to meet us afterwards. It's not safe out there, not any more.'Thérèse cast her eyes down, concealing a smile of satisfaction. 'All right, Maman, if you insist.'

# La Belote

'Ace takes all. My deal.' Albert gathered up the cards, tapped them down.

Marcel brought a heavy fist down on the waxed cloth. The kitchen table wobbled under the impact. 'That's five times you've trumped me, only the first round, too,' he grumbled. They glared at each other, implacable adversaries. The next moment, as if on cue, the confrontation gave place to an exchange of nods and grins, the easy complicity of veteran actors as they play out a long familiar performance.

Scores were duly recorded, then Marcel reached across the table for his packet of *Gauloises Bleues*. Not easy to come by, these days, but he deserved a treat to make up for his loss. Cigarette poised on the edge of his lips, he tapped the pockets of his jacket, frowning impatiently.

'*Tiens*! I've left my *briquet** at home. Give us a light, at least, to make up for your triumph, you conniving devil!'

Albert grunted an assent and started to rummage through his pockets, pulling out his pouch of *tabac gris** and some cigarette papers, then, with increasing frustration, extracting coils of string, shredded receipts from clients, an assortment of nails and a well worn *Opinel.** Marcel was about to intervene when a box of matches was placed in front of him.

'Ah, many thanks, Madame Griot,' he said, looking up with a smile. 'You always seem to know what's wanted, don't you?'

There was no answer to that. Lucette seated herself by the fire, extracting her knitting from the sewing basket. After all these evenings of *belote*,* she still found herself on edge with Marcel Richaud. Perhaps it was that hint of insinuation in his manner, or merely the way he looked at her, one way or another, it set her pulse going to an uncomfortable degree.

She shifted in her armchair, willingly turning her attention to the task in hand. Claude's jumper was barely started, she needed to get on and finish it soon; the one he was wearing now was such a struggle to pull over his head. It was a pleasure to set the needles clicking, to become absorbed in the rhythm of the work.

Marcel Richaud was a good friend of the family, she reminded herself, counting stitches as the yarn unravelled. Why worry about his behaviour when she had so much worse to cope with in her daily life.

German soldiers would bash on the door to shove bundles of laundry at her, gabbing like geese! It was a struggle to get any sense out of them. Heinrich was an exception, always polite, at least he made an effort to speak French properly.

Nicolas could do a perfect imitation of a Franco-German accent, Albert had to warn the child not to try it again, they'd all be in trouble if it was overheard.

Through a haze of smoke she glanced across at the game in progress. An oil lamp stationed on the sideboard cast an amber glow over the card table, outlined the shadowy forms of the hunched players. There was much frowning over fans of cards cushioned in calloused hands, heavy silences of ponderous deliberation. Play was cautious and considered, as though their livelihoods were at stake.

With a benign smile she resumed counting stitches. The floor creaked overhead, Thérèse was moving about in her room. She'd be on her knees, soon, at her prayers, before she settled into bed.

Lucette felt her heart expand. This sense of contentment and peace, perhaps it was something like happiness? If only time would stop right now, they could remain here forever, warm and secure. She could delude herself that the world outside was of no account: the threatening notices posted up in the street, the German soldiers in their grey uniforms, the food coupons, requisitions, shortages, the *marché gris\**, making do. None of it mattered now.

The sound of knuckles cracking made her wince. Albert was stretching his arms out, yawning, the end of a game. 'I'd say it's time for me to hit the sack, it's been a long day.'

Marcel lifted his eyebrows in surprise as he surveyed his partner. 'Oh come on, Albert, let's have another round. It's not anywhere near curfew yet.'

'No, I've had enough, really.' Albert was pushing the cards away, 'almost forgot I've got a double shift starting tomorrow night: new schedule.'

'They're becoming aware of your inestimable merits,' Marcel responded, in humorous vein.

Albert snorted. 'I never thought they'd rope in an old guy like me for Obligatory Work Service.'[5] He cast an envious glance at Marcel. 'You should count yourself lucky, getting let off like you did.'

'Oh, they'll be after me soon enough,' Marcel reassured him, 'only a question of time.' He stacked the cards with care, recalling the trick he'd pulled off when the last summons came through. Three aspirin, crushed into a cigarette. It was Menier's tip, worked like a charm. 'You'll soon be standing on the platform waving as the train to Munich or Essen shunts past,' he continued, 'that is, unless they find something else for you to do.'

'Not likely,' Albert replied. 'Seems to have become a permanent fixture now, railway surveillance. With Surdon Junction so close by, they're hardly likely to let us off. Just think about it: Paris, Granville, Rouen, Tours, they all connect from there. The Boche are not going to be taking any chances.'

Marcel nodded. 'No wonder you're turning in early. You veteran troopers need your shut eye, eh?'

'It's as good an excuse as any, now you mention it.' Albert heaved himself up, yawning. His eyes crinkled with amusement. 'You know the old saying, better to quit while the going's good. The score is just about even for now, but I'm well aware that you're biding your time, you crafty bugger!'

Marcel grinned as he scraped his chair back, levering himself into a vertical position. 'Sussed me out, as usual. I'll let you off, this time round, but you wait and see. The revenge match will be sensational.'

Lucette was intent on her knitting, but surely within earshot. He was careful to adopt a casual tone as he tried to establish which shifts Albert was working during the next week.

'Monday, Wednesday and Friday, same as usual,' came the response.

Marcel drew closer, speaking in an undertone. 'Word's going round that there's likely to be some activity on your stretch of track.' Albert raised his eyebrows, gripping the back of the chair.

'If you've got any choice in the matter,' Marcel continued, 'you could opt for a Wednesday off, just for next week.' He tried not to flinch under Albert's steady gaze. 'You wouldn't want to witness anything going on, know what I mean?'

Albert stood, motionless, frowning at the table. Marcel began to regret having spoken. 'Just thought I'd better mention it. Only a rumour but you never know.'

The silence was palpable. As if coming to a decision, Albert pulled the chair out, gesturing towards Marcel. 'Thanks. Why not stay on for a bit? No need to turf you out just because I'm having an early night.'

Marcel let out his breath. 'I couldn't possibly. . .'

'Go on, sit down. Lucette will make you some coffee.' Albert was on his way out before Marcel could come up with any excuses.

He sat on the edge of the chair, mulling over the exchange. He'd been too explicit about avoiding Wednesday. Albert would realise that he was involved, or at least had some contact with resistance activity. But was his reluctant acquiescence a sign of suspicious hostility or implicit sympathy? The invitation to stay on, could it be interpreted as a token of solidarity? So hard to tell with an inscrutable chap like that. He wanted to be alone now, to give himself time to think.

He turned towards Lucette, ready to make his excuses at the first opportunity. She was busily occupied, rolling up her knitting. He cleared his throat, picked up his cap. As if on cue, the work basket was set aside, she was on her feet, moving towards him.

'Albert wouldn't want you to go before you've had a cup. There's a pot on the stove, it won't take a moment.' With a polite smile, she vanished through the kitchen door. It seemed there was no other option.

He sat down, again, tapping his fingers on his thigh, thoughts spinning, until the swish of a skirt announced her return. She set the tray down between them. Lifting the brown enamel pot, she poured a steaming stream into each cup.

'It's just the usual barley and chicory mix,' she apologised, 'I can't even offer you saccharine, this time. Perhaps you'd like a drop of Calvados in it?'

'Please don't bother, it's quite all right.' Banishing the last twinges of restlessness, he accepted the proffered cup with polite solemnity. 'I'll take it as it comes, with grateful thanks, Madame Griot. And please, do call me Marcel.'

Lucette flushed, picked up a teaspoon, stirred her coffee. 'Monsieur Richaud, I could hardly presume . . .' She kept her eyes on the swirling drink.

Marcel was beginning to enjoy his enforced stay. He leaned back in the chair, sipping the brew at his leisure. The mellow glow of lamplight seeped into the encroaching darkness. He followed the play of light across her features: cheekbone, forehead, chin, softly illuminated. She was gazing at the dwindling fire, now, her brow creased in thought.

He lit a cigarette, smoked in silence, waiting for her to speak. After a few minutes, she set her cup down, leaned forward to stir the embers, coaxing them into life again. Satisfied, she turned to face him.

'There is something I'd like to ask you, if you don't mind, Monsieur Rich. . .Marcel?'

'I'm at your service.'

She cast her eyes down, hesitating. 'I couldn't help overhearing some of your conversation with Albert, you know, when you were asking

58

about his night shifts. . . '

Marcel shifted in his chair, regretting ill-timed words of warning. He was soon able to relax again. Lucette merely wanted to hear about Albert's duties, judging by the nature of the questions she was asking. For one reason or another, Albert hadn't bothered to illuminate her. 'There's nothing wrong with knowing what he does, is there?' she demanded. 'It's not confidential, is it?'

'No, of course not,' Marcel reassured her, 'but I'm hardly the best person . . .'

'He won't talk about it, gets angry if I ask. Last week I tried to find out when he was coming home and . .' She looked away, biting her lip.

Marcel began to wonder what went on between them. Surely Albert wouldn't lift a hand against her? He would need to choose his words carefully, to do what he could to ease her anxieties, without dropping hints that he was involved with the local cell group.

'I know it must be rotten for Albert, working for the Germans,' he began, 'that's probably the reason he doesn't want to talk about it. But at least it's not slave labour in a German munitions factory. Older fellows don't get sent away, more luck to them. As a younger chap, I could be packed off tomorrow.'

Her eyes opened wide with concern. 'Oh, I do hope not. Madame Bourrier told me they came for her son last week. He was frogmarched onto a train that very same day . .' She gazed at the fire with an air of perplexity, then turned to face Marcel.

'I still don't understand. Why do you think they've put him on railway patrol? It's not as if a saddler would know anything about trains; there seem to be more and more shifts all the time.' She lowered her voice. 'I've heard about the Resistance, of course, do you think they might have plans to sabotage the railway lines near us?' Marcel glanced away, trying to conceal his surprise at the accuracy of her thoughts. Responding with an exaggerated shrug, he spread his hands.

'No idea. I've heard reports that the Resistance have stepped up their operations recently; hardly surprising that the Boche are getting worried.' His tone became confidential. 'Remember the incident at Ecouché last month?'

The pause was momentary. 'You mean the train that was derailed? So that was. . .'

'It wasn't an accident. They found a whole section of track missing.' He could tell by her expression that she was making all the right connections. 'Now that it's been mended the Boche want to keep it going.'

'That would explain the extra shifts,' she concluded, 'they couldn't care less about his experience.'

She was twisting the skin of her wrists, now, staring at the rug beneath their feet. 'If he's on patrol to prevent Resistance operations, they'll expect him to . . .' Her voice choked. 'How he can bear to do it, I simply don't understand? There might be people we know out there, taking part in these activities, risking their lives!' Suddenly she was on her feet, eyes blazing as she confronted him.

'My husband out there night after night helping the Germans! Making targets of our own people!' She turned towards the fire, fists clenched tight, then drew them to her cheeks, pressing into the bone.

Marcel stood up, suddenly aware of an unaccountable desire to fold her into his arms. He took a deep breath, exhaling slowly. After a few moments he placed his hand on her shoulder. 'Easy does it,' he said, as he watched his fingers travel down her arm, stroking her sleeve. He could feel the taut muscles beginning to ease. She drew away, sank down into her chair.

Words of empty reassurance found their way to his lips. 'It won't come to that, believe me.' He swallowed hard. 'I'm sure he's there for surveillance work, that's all.' The chair creaked in accusation as he sat down again. Sceptical eyes were trained on his face.

He leaned forward, determined to persuade her. 'Think about the location of Surdon Junction. Albert and his mates patrol a five kilometre stretch either side, isn't that so? Any Resistance group must be well aware of the timetable, the routine, the limits – they've all got their sources. If they want to sabotage the line, surely they'll be finding a spot where it's less likely they'll be caught?'

He leaned back, crossing his arms. 'Albert won't be seeing much activity on his rounds, believe me.' Wishful thinking, perhaps.

Her face softened. 'I hope you're right.' She lowered her head. 'Otherwise, it hardly bears thinking about.'

There was no answer to that. After a long silence, he drew himself up, shifted his weight. 'I really ought to be on my way.'

She glanced at the clock on the shelf, clapped a hand over her mouth. '*Tiens*! Long past curfew! I'm so sorry, keeping you here with all my worries.'

'It's no problem at all. I'll go out through the back door. The Boche don't make a habit of patrolling the lane behind your house.'

Standing on the threshold, he felt the light pressure of her hand on his arm. 'Thank you for listening. . . Marcel.'

He turned round, his gaze searching, looked away, rotating the cap in his hands. Finally, he positioned it on his head, pulling it firmly down.

A dog barked somewhere in the darkness. Marcel buttoned his jacket, turned up the collar. 'You'll let me know if there's anything else I can do, won't you? He stepped into the yard.

From the depths of the house, the cry of a child started up. The door closed behind him.

# FEBRUARY – APRIL 1944

# Puncture

The bicycle was upended in the workshop, a tyre hanging off the rim of the front wheel. Albert stooped over a basin of water, a dripping inner tube in his hands. He grinned at Marcel. 'Puncture.' he pronounced, with the confident air of a person who enjoys solving practical problems. 'Thought I'd sorted it, only to discover an old patch had come unstuck. Whoever had this bike before me made a right botch of it.'

Marcel sniffed, wrinkling his nose. 'So that's why the place is reeking of Secotine⁶, smells like last week's fish.' He picked up the limp end of the inner tube, inspecting. 'Where the deuce did you get hold of it? I've been making a regular nuisance of myself at Didier's shop trying to get one: went over to Sées, to Argentan, it's like asking for gold dust, complete waste of time. Had to make do with solid tyres for the last six months.'

Albert tipped his head, gave him a knowing wink. 'Should have asked me, could have got you one in Paris, no problem.'

Marcel surveyed him with respect. The old boy certainly knew how to work the system. 'Been on the circuit again, have you?'

Albert grunted an affirmation as he flattened the tube out on the workbench. 'Just a little excursion, you might say, to make sure my sources are still reliable. It's easier to get the bicycle stamps⁷ from Madame Brionne at this time of year; not so much competition for them.'

He squeezed a trickle of Secotine over the punctured area, then lit a match, holding it close to the glistening glue, blowing hard, until the flare of flame was extinguished.

'After all, it helps everyone,' he continued, pressing a rubber patch onto the vulcanised spot. He ran the edge of his thumb round it. 'George has got plenty of clients in Montmartre for my home grown tobacco. He was pleased to be on the receiving end, I'll tell you that.'

'They know when they're on to a good thing,' Marcel confirmed. 'You wouldn't believe some of the stuff I've been offered. Laced with dried sunflower leaves, Jerusalem artichoke, God knows what else!'

'You don't say,' Albert replied, gazing at the wall. After a moment he cast a canny look in Marcel's direction. 'Yes, it's not bad, my little blend. In demand, at any rate, got rid of the lot.' He gave a satisfied sigh. 'My little parcel of butter went down well, too. I was able to come back with everything I was after and more. Well worth the trip.'

Marcel hung his shoulder bag on a peg behind the door. 'Resourceful as always, Albert. Let me know next time you go, I'll order a supply of truffles.'

Albert chuckled as he held the tube up, inspecting. 'Good as new, I'd say.'

Marcel checked his watch. 'I'd better give you a hand fitting it back in place. You've still got a shift tonight, haven't you? It would take me a good twenty minutes to get to the station at Surdon, you're not going to tell me that you can do it in less!' Albert shot him a sideways glance. 'Never been late yet, but I certainly won't say no, seeing as you're on the spot. Been cutting it a bit fine lately, got to admit.'

'Not worth the risk, Albert, if you don't mind me saying. I hear that's how your friend Arnaud got into trouble.'

'Poor old sod! That day he staggered into the depot, at least half and hour late he was, hobbling along like an old man. Made some joke about how he had one too many and tripped up on his doorstep.'

'That's a good one! Odette told me he'd taken a short cut through the fields and stepped on a rabbit trap.'

Albert nodded, sagely. 'Might be so. Didn't want to admit he'd been so careless, can't blame him.'

Marcel was rolling his sleeves up. 'Arnaud's wife wasn't too happy about it. They had their ration coupons cancelled for the rest of the month.'

'At least they didn't pack him off to Hamburg,' Albert remarked, moving into position next to the bicycle.

Marcel rubbed his hands together. 'Ready for action?'

Between the two of them, the bicycle was soon re-assembled. Albert inflated the tyre and turned it right side up, leaning the bike against the wall. Wiping his hands on a rag, he started for the kitchen, gesturing Marcel to follow. 'We'll have a bit of a clean up in the yard.'

The kitchen was buzzing with sounds of activity: the clatter of crockery, water splashing in the scullery, voices calling out. A pot on the stove bubbled, emitting a mouth-watering aroma of chicken and leek.

Through the open door of the scullery he could see Lucette chatting to Thérèse in the ritual of washing up, drying, stacking, a swirling white tea towel much in evidence. It was an intrusion, entering the realm of these women. He tried to slip past, but Lucette had already registered the startled look on her daughter's face.

'What's got into you?' she demanded, before her turned glance took on an equal measure of confusion. 'Monsieur Richaud!'

Marcel hastened to make amends with a profuse greeting, gesturing an apology with grease-covered hands.

'It's no problem at all,' Lucette responded, poised in the entrance to the scullery, a casserole lid lifted like a gleaming shield between them.

Thérèse held a stack of plates to her chest, murmuring apologies as she threaded her way past. Albert was already through the back door.

'Please don't let me interrupt your work.' Marcel drew away, eager to follow in his footsteps.

Typical of the old boy to organise his overnight visit without telling the women. Lucette seemed ill at ease. Ever since that late night conversation in November, something had changed. She never seemed to be around, much, when he came over to play *Belote* of an evening. She'd offer a cordial welcome when she answered the door, but there'd been an underlying sense of constraint he hadn't noticed before. He stepped out into the yard, frowning. If it was something to do with her marriage, it was none of his business.

Albert was standing in the entrance to the laundry room, pouring water into a tin basin. A few words were sufficient to confirm the status quo; the women would be finding out soon enough, that was all that mattered to him.

'Don't you worry, there'll be no complaints,' Albert assured him, rubbing a scrap of soap into calloused hands. 'Lucette has been on at me day in day out, fretting about being left on her own to cope. Now that I've done something about it, she should be satisfied.'

'I'm only too pleased to help out. Sharing sleeping quarters with Laurence was fine while we were growing up, but it's a bit more of a squeeze these days in the Richaud household. As long as your women really don't mind, that's all I'm thinking of.'

Albert grunted a reply. 'They can put up with you for the time being, no fear. If you're going to be packed off to Germany, might as well make use of you while you're still around.'

'You've made the right decision,' Marcel said, drying his hands on the coarse linen towel Albert tossed over to him. 'I expect you've heard about some of those recent incidents in Rouen. Women on their own are at risk these days, no doubt about it.'

'Hum! Even so, at the end of the day, women will always find something to fuss about.'

Thérèse had disappeared by the time they got back. Lucette, her composure restored, was unrolling the sleeves of her dress. She shot an enquiring glance at Albert. 'You've got a guest tonight,' he announced, as he shouldered the jacket from the back of a chair. 'I'll be off, now, see you tomorrow.' He was already heading towards the door.

Lucette opened her mouth, but didn't speak. After a few moments, she moved towards the stove.

'Perhaps you'd like to sit down, I can offer you some chicory coffee.'

Marcel pulled out a chair, hesitating. 'Are you sure it's all right?'

She picked up a cup from the sideboard, turning it in her hands. 'What do you mean?'

'Is it all right with you, me stopping over?' The arrangement needed to be clarified, he could see that now. 'Albert told me he'd feel reassured if I could stay here when he does night shifts. But I could easily go home, no problem.'

'It's perfectly all right,' she said, pouring coffee. She met his eyes, offering the cup. 'In any case, it's not up to me.'

Thérèse came back, a pre-occupied look on her face. Seated at last, he tried not to listen to the furtive consultation between the two of them. It soon came to an end. Lucette gave a warm smile, patting the girl's arm as she sent her on her way.

She turned to Marcel, saying 'As Francine has gone back to Paris, we're making up the bed in her old room, it shouldn't take long.'

The constraint in her manner could only be met with equal politeness. 'How very kind of you. Is there something I can do to help?' He was already on his feet, moving around the room in restless anticipation. Once she was able to adjust to his presence, he'd be on firm ground again.

The wood basket by the stove was nearly depleted. 'I'll take care of this,' he announced, taking possession, heading for the door. He could already tell that he was going to enjoy his new duties.

# Before Curfew

'We've got plenty of time,' Laurence said, stroking her hand. 'Curfew's not for another hour.'

Thérèse met his eyes with an expectant smile, letting him steer her away from the kitchen door to a secluded corner behind the laundry room. This time she allowed him to unbutton her coat, quivering as his hands slid gently across her chest, moving down to encircle her waist, pulling her close. The heat of his body was melting her like wax, kindling secret parts of her anatomy, churning and turning them inside out. This couldn't be right. She pulled back, panic-stricken, placed a restraining hand on his chest. It pulsed with his urgent breath.

'We can't, Laurence, you know that. Not yet.'

He brushed her hand away, exasperated. 'Why should we go on waiting?' The next moment, her hand was recaptured, insistent fingers rubbing her palm, reining her in.

'Come on, Thérèse, it can't make all that much difference. You want to, I can tell you do, you can't deny it. I'll keep you warm, don't worry.'

She looked away, eyes brimming with tears as she fumbled to disengage herself.

A shadow crossed his face. He scowled, stepped back. 'Don't you trust me?'

'Oh, Laurence, you know that's not . . .'

'You do love me, don't you?'

She felt a lump in her throat as she nodded, reaching out to caress his cheek, her eyes entreating. Surely he would understand? She smiled, reassured, as Laurence seized her hand to plant soft kisses on her fingers and wrist, gently pulling her into an embrace.

'Well then, why wait any longer? It's been two years now, hasn't it, since we met? I knew, almost from the start, that you and I were destined for each other.' He buried his face in her hair, murmuring, 'No other woman exists for me. I think about you every single day, treasure every moment we can be together.' His lips brushed her ear. 'Isn't that enough evidence for you?'

She rested her forehead on his shoulder, finally drawing away, taking both of his hands in hers.

'I'll be eighteen next month, Laurence. You know that Papa made me promise to wait until then to get married. Surely it's not much to ask?' She faltered, seeing his features darken. Tears coursed down her cheeks, unheeded.

He pulled away, again, turning to punch his fist into his palm as he muttered under his breath. Still not ready for him. It seemed an eternity before he was able to coax her into his arms again, gently wiping her eyes with the back of his hand. She swallowed the sobs shaking her frame. Why could he not understand? Their love, their special love deserved the endorsement of a sanctified rite, not some furtive consummation in a barn or back alley.

Darkness thickened the privet hedge beyond them. A window rattled upstairs, setting the hens clucking in their coop. She rested her head against his shoulder, trying to collect her thoughts. If she could only explain the situation properly, he would understand. Of course he would.

'All I am asking, Laurence, is for us to wait a little longer. We can be married, soon.' It was the right thing to do, she wanted to add, to go to her marriage bed in a state of purity. The image of a woman lying face down in a huge bed invaded her consciousness. Naked, covered to the waist by a long white sheet. Laurence knelt beside the bed, peeling the sheet away, little by little, bending over to kiss the newly revealed flesh. She flushed crimson at the audacity of her imagination.

Laurence continued to plead with her, his voice low, urgently persuasive. 'You know we belong to each other, Thérèse. What's the point of waiting for some doddering old priest to pontificate about our union?'

A shower of cold water cascaded over them, drenching heads and shoulders. She gasped, cringing, as Laurence attempted to shield her with his arm, uttering expletives she didn't want to hear. Craning her neck to peer at the roof, she caught sight of Nicolas scrabbling over the tiles, hoisting himself through the gaping window of his bedroom.

'You little devil!' Laurence was shaking his fist at the boy. 'Wait till I get hold of you. You'll pay for this!'

She tugged his arm in supplication. 'Please, Laurence, he doesn't mean any harm. Let's not stir things up, it's only water, after all.' If Maman found out they'd been lingering in the garden, she'd never hear the end of it.

'Laurence brushed his jacket down, frowning, as he registered the implications of pursuit. 'Shouldn't get away with it, that little horror.'

'I'll speak to him tomorrow,' she promised, in resolute tones, 'leave it to me.'

In the kitchen, Marcel was seated at the table, gazing at her mother, as if in a trance. Taking note of her arrival, he flashed his habitual, insinuating smile. This time it was almost reassuring. Now he was rising to greet her, overtly polite. She turned away to close the door.

Maman was on her feet, restlessly moving about the kitchen, a litany of worried complaints streaming from her. It was some relief to be able to respond in kind.

'It's Saturday night, Maman. I've been to see Laurence, as I always do.'

'You shouldn't stay out so late, I was beginning to worry about you.'

Hardly likely, Thérèse considered, wondering why such an uncharitable notion had popped into her head. And really, there was enough anxiety in the querulous voice to stir her remorse.

'I'm sorry, Maman, I lost track of time.'

Maman was equally contrite. 'Never mind, *cherie*. You usually see him on a Saturday, I should have remembered.'

Thérèse hung her coat on the back of the kitchen door. She glanced again at Marcel, polishing the table with his thumb, humming, tunelessly. If Maman had been on her own, she'd have settled down beside her with a hot drink, for a cosy session recounting her evening adventures. Some of them, at any rate. It wasn't going to happen tonight.'I'm off to bed,' she announced, giving her mother a perfunctory kiss.

Maman was a model of solicitude as she offered soup, warm drinks, finally producing a hot brick from the bottom of the oven to envelop in a tea towel. 'At least it will take the chill off,' she insisted.

Clutching the warm bundle against her chest, Thérèse caught a glimpse of them just before the door closed. Their eyes, locked together.

# At Madame Foularde's

The Samson was on its way – he could hear the muffled roar gaining intensity as the automobile jolted over potholes on the Grande Rue. Menier, off on his rounds again, he knew without even turning round. Apart from the Mercedes belonging to *Kommandant Kroger*, it was the only car in circulation. The doctor made full use of his professional status to extract a generous petrol allowance from the Germans, there was no other way to keep it going. It was probably to his advantage that they happened to like him as well.

The long sleek automobile shuddered to a halt as it drew level with him. A close-cropped head emerged, weather-beaten features framed by the open window. An exchange of greetings was in order.

'On your way to the printers?'

'Yes, got to be heading back. Old Monsieur Dambert keeps me on the straight and narrow.' Marcel felt the grip on his hand tighten, reining him in.

'I'll be paying a visit to old Madame Foularde this afternoon. She's a bit under the weather.' It took only a moment to register the doctor's intent. Marcel met his gaze with a nod. 'You might just happen to drop by after work this evening, see if she needs any help.'

'Of course. With pleasure.'

It was becoming an arrangement as familiar as an evening tipple at Odette's. There were just a few trustworthy patients Menier could rely on; Madame Foularde was tried and tested. Marcel stepped back, lifted his cap and waved as the car roared off.

The shift took longer than usual, no time to wash the ink off his hands. He set off at a brisk pace across the Place Centrale and continued along the Grande Rue toward the outskirts of town.

Several off-duty German soldiers sauntered towards him, unable to resist coming out with a few jibes as he passed by. 'You'd better get a move on, mate, she won't hang about waiting for the likes of you.' He humoured them with an inane grin, it always worked.

The Samson was parked just outside Madame Foularde's modest brick dwelling, the mud-spattered tyres and bonnet evidence of the doctor's rounds for the day. Marcel slowed to an ambling pace, glanced both ways, before slipping down a side alley to make his approach through the back garden. Menier could leave his car anywhere and get away with it; the rest of them had to take more care.

A signal tapped on in the door gained admittance to a dark cavern of a kitchen, filled with smoke. André and Henri huddled over an oilcloth covered table, deep in consultation with Menier, while Madame Foularde poured out drinks from a cracked enamel pot, real coffee, it seemed, judging by the aroma wafting towards him. She offered a cup to Robert, holding him captive with a detailed account of the state of her knees. Robert shifted from one foot to the other, politely attentive. Catching sight of Marcel, she broke off her monologue to greet him with a broad smile. Her eyes were sparkling as she brandished the coffee pot. Not much wrong with her.

'*Bienvenue monsieur*! Let me pour you a cup.'

He sipped at her brew with genuine appreciation. 'It's many a month since I've tasted the real stuff, Madame Foularde, you're too kind.'

'Not at all, sir, none of my doing. It's the good doctor who brings it to me, so considerate, he is. Can't imagine where he manages to get hold of the stuff, but it's not for me to ask. We must take our blessings as they come.' She winked at him, moving on.

The last cup dispensed, the old woman hovered by the stove until Menier had a few words to thank her on their behalf. André held the door while she shuffled out.

The doctor pulled a tightly folded paper from an inside pocket of his jacket. He smoothed it out on the table, his expression intently focused.

'OK lads, here's the latest. Picked up a message from London last night. The next parachute drop is scheduled for midnight on Tuesday. Dropping zone: the field just beyond St. Hilaire chapel.'

His news provoked an outburst of exchanges. Menier cleared his throat. 'I suggest we meet at the edge of the wood nearest the dropping zone, 23:30 sharp. Make sure you've got a torch. Once they get rid of the canisters, it's up to us to sort them out as quickly as we can; you know the ropes. I've been told it's going to be about the same quantity as last time: Bren guns, Sten sub-machine guns, ammunition, emergency provisions.'

'Where are we going to stash it?' Robert asked.

'The farm at Vaudiéres. There's still plenty of room in the barn there.' His sharp gaze travelled around the room. 'I'm counting on all four of you to turn up without fail. Have you got any questions?'

Henri launched in with the usual obsessive round of concerns. How many boxes were there? How many hours did Menier anticipate they'd need to wait? What were the Huns up to on Tuesday nights, had the check points been changed since last time? What if it rained or the plane dropped the goods somewhere else? Marcel frowned with impatience, exchanging looks with Robert. These were all issues which had been discussed and resolved many times before.

Muttering protests started up, silenced by a cautionary gesture from Menier, who took pains to respond to every one of Henri's questions with elaborate patience. Was he worried about Henri's commitment? His loyalty? It would be the end of the line for all of them all if that man betrayed them.

They'd managed to avoid detection last time, lying low for a couple of months during the winter, while rumours were circulating. Menier had succeeded in keeping them up to date: almost miraculous that his radio hadn't been confiscated yet. The Boche must have turned a blind eye at some point, deliberately omitting the doctor's house from their searches. He might not be so lucky next time.

Menier was ready to lead them on to the next subject. 'The good news is that we've got two more recruits for our cell. I've made contact with a couple of *refractaires** hiding out in Écouves Forest; they've promised to give us a hand shifting the goods on Tuesday. We need to...'

'Yes, but who are they, how do we know we can trust them?' Henri interrupted.

'As you know, with the exception of myself, we're using pseudonyms here,' Menier responded, patiently. 'Let's call the first one Luke. He's been keeping a low profile for almost a year, now, ever since the Germans started cracking down on anyone with a Jewish background, however remote. No yellow badge for him, he insists.'

'I think I know who it is,' said André, 'if you're talking about a local. I never realised he was Jewish, though. It was his father who used to set up the crèche in the church every year.'

'Should have been obvious, if you'd looked at his features,' Henri muttered. 'It's the nose that gives them away.'

'When I was a kid,' André went on, immersed in his reflections, 'I used to go round to his house after school. His mother was always feeding us: dumplings, chicken soup, noodle pudding. . . I'm getting hungry again at the thought of it.'

'You're giving us all an appetite,' Menier responded, with a thin smile, before turning back to Henri. 'The other recruit has been working on the Colombier farm near Macé; he became a *refractaire* after the last Relève. For our purposes we'll call him Richard. He's another one who tried to forge his date of birth on his identity papers and thought he

72

could get away with it.'

'Bad luck,' Robert responded, 'he must be kicking himself!'

Henri gave a snort. 'Idiot! Should have known better. No wonder the Huns are after his hide.'

'You can rely on them both, take my word for it,' Menier continued, fixing his gaze on Henri. 'At this stage of the game you can trust me to sniff out an informer.'

Expressions of approval sounded from the group, reinforcing his words. Menier was on his feet now. 'Time we got going, don't want you lot getting into trouble for missing curfew. We'll stagger our exits, as usual. Henri, André, I suggest you slip away now.'

Marcel was heading for the door when he felt a tap on his shoulder. 'Thanks Robert, see you soon. I've got to have a word with Lucien, now.'

Left on their own, Menier crumpled his notes into a ball and fed it into the wood-fired stove. They stood watching the flames flare up.

'We've got Henri on board,' Menier remarked, as he slid the iron lid back into position, 'we can count on him for the time being.'

'I'll keep an eye on him if you like,' Marcel offered. Was that the reason he'd been asked to stay behind?

Menier reached under the table to retrieve the battered leather case he used on his rounds. A litre sized brown bottle was produced and set on the table with an air of satisfaction.

'Quite a substantial dose for our patient. Let's just make sure it's up to scratch, shall we?' Taken aback, Marcel watched him pour a dollop into each of their coffee cups. The unmistakable aroma of well-aged Calvados wafted towards him.

'Come on!' Menier urged, his cup raised in encouragement.

'*A votre santé*', Marcel responded, in cautious acknowledgement. The doctor had never singled him out as a drinking partner before.

'Better than a dose of quinine!' Menier sighed with satisfaction, moving on to extol the quality and provenance. 'Courtesy of a grateful patient in Sées. Her husband buried a case in the cellar during the 1914-18 war. Then died. Took her all this time to remember it was still down there!'

'Madame Foularde will be very pleased with your gift, I'm sure,' Marcel said, trying not to sound doubtful.

Menier spluttered, the cup clattered as it was set down. He pulled out a handkerchief to wipe his face, eyes crinkling with mirth. 'Actually, she can't stand the stuff. I've promised her a couple of boxes of sugar lumps next time I get hold of some. The point is, I can rely on her to keep it safe, along with the rest of the quality goods.'

He leaned closer, his tone becoming confidential. 'I do keep a few bottle of cheap rubbish at my place. Useful to bribe the Gestapo if they should happen to come round; they don't really know any better.' They both chuckled, as Menier poured out another round. 'Just a drop more before we set out.'

The double dose was beginning to take the edge off any lingering uneasiness. If the doctor wanted a drinking companion, he wasn't going to object. It wasn't until they were at the back door that Marcel began to have some idea what the convivial tête-a-tête with Menier was leading up to.

'Francine Griot called in at the surgery, last time she was in town.' Menier's hand rested on the latch. 'Hadn't seen her for a couple of years, lively as ever, isn't she! I heard about some of her adventures in Paris, she told me she could hardly wait to get back there.'

With a bland smile, Marcel offered words of approval, aware of a sinking sensation in the pit of his stomach. Any encounter with Francine usually spelled trouble. The latch clicked open. Menier waved him through, following hard on his heels.

Pulling the door shut behind them, Menier stopped, as if in contemplation of Madame Foularde's kitchen garden. 'I understand you've become quite a regular visitor to the Griot household.'

Marcel gave a nervous laugh, keeping his eyes trained on the garden gate.

'Yes, I do tend to drop round there more than I used to, Albert always appreciates it when I can give him a hand in the workshop, and of course we both enjoy a game of *Belote* of an evening when he's got time off. In fact, he was worried about the women being left on their own at night, asked me to stop over on those occasions, there seem to be more shifts laid on every week. Typical of the Boche, isn't it! '

He bit his lower lip, wishing he hadn't let his tongue run away with him. Obviously covering up for something, Menier would infer, even though all of it was true. What else had Francine said? She only stayed a week, but it was more than enough time to make mischief.

'Francine doesn't seem to like it when I'm there, the two of us never hit it off.' A lame excuse. He was digging himself into a hole. 'She told me to make myself scarce last time I turned up for Albert's evening shift; that was going one step too far, in my view.'

Menier gave a brisk laugh. 'That would explain it. Probably jealous of your status in the family, now that she's based in Paris.'

'Couldn't blame her for that.' They set off towards the gate. With any luck, the subject would be dropped.

An overgrown hawthorn lifted barbed branches across the path. Menier stepped to one side, turned to fix his gaze on Marcel, as if in sudden recollection. 'One thing I ought to mention. . .'

The compliant smile on Marcel's face tightened into a grimace. 'Francine told me that it seems to be her mother who finds you, shall we say, rather indispensable.' There was no mistaking his tone.

Marcel followed him to the gate, pouring out a stream of justifications to try to bluff his way. A woman like that left on her own so much and struggling to manage, he did what he could to assist, that's all. Albert had asked him to help out, how could he say no? As the gate creaked open, his excuses seemed to dissolve into the chill of early evening.

Menier gave a lop-sided smile, ushered him through. Turning to face the doctor, with apparent unconcern, Marcel offered the semblance of a shrug. His eyes were bleak. To lose Menier's trust would be the worst outcome he could imagine.

A slap on the back broke the tension in the air. The doctor gave a chuckle as he moved along.'You've certainly got a way with you, Marcel. Still, I'm hardly the one to call you to account.'

It was a timely reminder. Relief swept through Marcel like a new broom. He'd heard about the liaison between Menier and Madame Vampoule, the notary's wife. More than just a rumour, then.

A horde of children swarmed around the Samson. Nicolas and Xavier were grappling with each other, in competition for standing room on the dashboard; over-excited little girls scrawled ciphers on the dusty rear windows. The doctor scattered the children with a genial roar, threatening them with the perils they could anticipate for a missed curfew. He waited until they were out of sight before he confronted Marcel, his face set in cold severity.

'Just make sure you keep her completely out of it. No hints, no explanations, regardless of how much you think you can trust her. Walls have ears in a house like that.'

Marcel nodded, meeting his eyes. He stood still, watching the Samson until it was out of sight.

# Waiting

After the first hour, Lucette brought in an armful of logs from the shed, tipping a few into the stove. No use waiting any longer for him to fill up the basket. She cleared away the supper things, swept the floor. Thérèse had cramps again: she'd been packed off to bed clutching a towel-wrapped hot brick. There'd be more clearing up for her to do on her own, but she was glad of it. Much better to keep occupied, something to distract her from the grandfather clock ticking the minutes, sounding the hour in the silence of the night.

Chores accomplished, she hung her apron on the hook behind the door, settled by the stove with the sewing basket, overflowing with torn, worn garments in need of attention. She picked up one of Albert's socks, turned it inside out, with sceptical disdain. The heel was nearly gone but it might be worth salvaging.

With the new curfew times he'd be cautious, she told herself, perhaps waiting for the right moment to make his way to the house without being spotted. He'd know it wasn't worth running the risk of being seen. Martine's brother was stopped last week and hauled off to headquarters. They were still waiting for him to come home.

She could hear Claude, restless in his cot upstairs, whimpering, working up to a muffled wail. She bent over her work, trying to concentrate. He would never be able to settle down, again, if she went to him. The ball of wool was dwindling at a pace, time to look for another old jumper to unravel.

Marcel would be making his way up the lane at the back of the house by now, running his hand along the hidden contours of the gatepost, tracking the path through the pitch black garden. The dogs won't bark; they know him, but he'll tread carefully, wary of rousing the hens, anxious not to disturb the neighbours.

The crying upstairs began to subside, like a clock winding down. One sock done, inspected, rolled up; she couldn't stop herself glancing at the latch on the kitchen door again. Sometimes she'd notice the lever pushing up just before the hinge clicked.

She rummaged in the basket for the matching sock, a dull brown, so easy to mislay, turned it over in her hand. Much worse than the other, beyond repair, surely? In a spasm of petulance, she cast the sock aside, pushed the basket away to fold into herself, head cradling her hands.

A shooting pain spread across her temple, callipers squeezed the back of her head. This is what it will be like without him. Pain. Relentless suffocation. She balled her hands, pressing them into her neck. What did she think she was doing? A married woman, conducting an affair with her husband's friend, how could she have let it happen?

Shame flared a torch in her chest, heat rising, her cheeks burning. She pressed herself firmly into the back of the chair. It must come to an end. She'd break with him tonight, tell him how absurd it all was. Albert, with his notions, asking Marcel to stay in the house! What if he found out? Her shoulders began to quiver. Albert knows, or he will soon find out, that much is certain.

She swayed back and forth, covered her face. How could she begin to recover some semblance of a sense of proportion? A young man of twenty-four years; he should be looking out for a suitable woman to start a family with. Could she bear it if he did? The Occupation had stamped their union, endorsing her fate.

A cringing sense of guilt burrowed into her consciousness. How long was it since she'd been to confession? 'I'm off to see Father Benoît,' Thérèse would announce, casting her eyes down. She'd wait a few moments before turning away.

Lucette bit her lips, drawing them into her jaw, eyes screwed shut. Marcel would remain her own secret transgression. God knows, she was already punished enough for it.

On her way up to bed she caught the faint tread of hasty footsteps in the garden, the soft scrape of the kitchen door. She sank down on one of the steps to wipe her eyes, trying to compose herself. Depression, shame, remorse seemed to be ebbing away through every pore of her skin, vanishing into the shadows of the dark passageway.

Her step was buoyant as she entered the kitchen. He was on the bench by the door, struggling to unlace mud-caked boots. Glancing up, he gave a rueful smile. 'Sorry about the mess. I hope you didn't stay up on my account?'

She smoothed his wet hair down with a light touch, busied herself easing his jacket off, hanging it to dry on a chair by the stove.

'I'll see if there's any coffee left.' She knew she couldn't ask him where he'd been. Waiting by the stove she felt his arms encircle her waist, his chin nuzzling into her neck. He was here now, that's all that mattered.

# MAY 1944

# The Incident

He'd never known Marcel to come into the workshop without some sort of palaver. This time he marched in without so much as a by your leave, with a face like thunder, what's more, eyes staring as if he was still seeing it, whatever damn thing it was. A sure sign of one of his black moods coming on, he knew it. Albert bent over the halter he was working on, listening for the click of the inner door. The bolt grated into place. Marcel wasn't usually so security conscious, must be a new whim of his. A chair scraped on the flagstones, squeaking a protest at such decisive action.

He cast a quizzical glance at his friend and gave a brief nod, barely interrupting his task. This piece he was working on, nice bit of leather, though it was on the thick side. Could be a bonus, though, for a sturdy halter. The gimlet was working a treat after being sharpened, punching through the double layer with minimum resistance, making perfect holes for the tarred threads.

He fell back into the rhythm of his task: punching holes, setting the gimlet aside to pick up a needle in each hand. The tarred threads slid through with ease, his hands performing an intricate duet as the crossed stitches lengthened along the rim of the collar. He shifted on his stool, taking care to keep his knees gripped against the wooden pincers wedged between his legs. If he let them slip, the gimlet holes wouldn't line up properly. Couldn't afford to get sloppy at this stage.

The chair creaked again. Marcel was trying to roll a cigarette; he seemed to be all left thumbs today. Flakes of *tabac gris* peppered the floor around them.

'*Merde*! Wretched stuff, tastes like shit and crumbles to dust!'

Albert waved his gimlet at the workbench. 'Have a go at mine, help yourself.' He pushed into the leather again, levering the tool with his palm. Much easier this time, must be thinning out, this end of the hide.

When Marcel had something on his mind, you could always tell, no two ways about it. He heaved a deep sigh as he pulled the next stitch through. If his friend had something to tell him, he'd come out with the news soon enough, no need to hurry it along.

The next time he looked around, Marcel was leaning towards him, evidently working himself up to a confidential moment. But then, all he said was, 'Have you got a shift tomorrow?'

'Of course! What are you talking about?' Albert shook his head.

'Come off it, mate, you know when my shifts are.'

The lad must be losing his grip, forgetting what day it was, perhaps he'd better put him straight? 'Tomorrow is Thursday, in case you've forgotten. I take it you'll still be able to stop here overnight?'

Marcel frowned at a harness hanging from the wall. Going deaf as well, so it seemed.

One last stitch and he could draw the threads tight and trim the ends. Finished at last, he set the halter aside and let the wooden brace slide away. Marcel must be scheming to get off with some young floozy, can't be bothered to keep his promises to an old friend.

Albert swivelled round, stone faced, to stow away the brace under the workbench. 'If you've got something else to do, we'll manage. Don't you worry about us!'

'It's not that . . .'

'You certainly won't catch me skiving off my shift! The Boche are cracking down even harder now, what with the *Résistance-Fer* * sabotaging the trains and the FFL hijacking goods whenever they can. Anyone not turning up becomes a partisan as far as. . .'

The boy was getting hot under the collar now. 'Albert, for Christ Sake, listen to me! Haven't you heard what's going on? Just down the road here, too, I can hardly believe. . .'

'Some of us are too busy to spend time gossiping.' That should put him in his place. He cleared the workbench, making space for the halter. Taking up a rag, he began to wipe smears of tar from the leather. A grudging curiosity got the better of him. 'What have the Krauts been up to now?'

'Not them, not this time!' Marcel replied, as if the qualification would improve the situation. 'It's Bernard, this time he's got himself into big trouble.'

'Bernard! Trust him to fall foul of the Boche! Has he had another set to with Trauber?' He rubbed the fading imprint of the gimlet in the hollow of his hand. Bernard should learn to button his lip with his drinking cronies, keep his hands in his pockets. With the Germans, it's best to ignore the barrage of insults you come up against, keep mum, that's the only way to survive.

Marcel was in full spate now, almost tripping over his words. '. . . you must have noticed how he's been getting quite matey with some of the Germans recently, even after falling out with Trauber. No harm keeping on the right side of them, I'm all for it, only Bernard doesn't know where to draw the line. A few drinks with Stimmer, one thing leads to another and before you know it the most . . . '

'Which one is Stimmer, for Christ's sake? They all look the same to me.'

'The red-faced one with the moustache. Some of the officers have been using him as a chauffeur, you must have seen him.'

It was the hands that came to mind, leathery hands stroking the gleaming surface of the Mercedes, making a show of polishing the chrome bumper. He'd chat to anyone willing to stop, trying to crack jokes with the local girls.

'Bit of a slacker, for a Boche, I'd say. Nicolas used to hang round him, trying to cadge cigarettes. I soon put a stop to that when I heard what was going on, no fear.'

'Just as well, but listen to this. Yesterday, at Bernard's, the two of them were having a couple of drinks, in the yard at the back of the house. Somehow or other, they got into an argument. Bernard knocked him over the head with a bottle; the chap tumbled over backwards onto the broken wheel of a cart. The metal axle pierced his skull.'

'Christ!' So that was the news. Albert staggered to his feet, staring at the ground as he tried to take it in. It took a few moments before he could meet Marcel's eyes. ' Poor bloke! What a way to go, for anyone!'

'Let's hope he was put out of his misery straight away.' Marcel was ready to move on. 'Bernard goes into panic mode, thinks he'd better cover up. What does he do? There's a bread oven at the back of the yard, cold, empty, fit for purpose. He hauls him into it. The wife turns up in time to help, you know what an Amazon she is. He might be small, our Bernard, but he makes up for it in resourcefulness.'

'Enterprising, if nothing else,' Albert leaned back against the workbench and crossed his arms. 'Well, you've got to admit it's original.'

'So then, wouldn't you know, Stimmer's mate comes along. Catches them stuffing kindling into the oven, the feet still poking out, blood blazing a trail right up to them.'

Albert shook his head, dolefully. 'A sad business. I knew that Bernard would get himself into trouble, again, sooner or later. It never would have crossed my mind that it could be as bad as that!'

Marcel was pacing the room now. What next? 'If you think that's the end of the story, you'd better think again,' he burst out with, coming to a halt. ' Bernard will be executed, possibly his wife as well, the rest of us forced to witness the event.'

'Like that poor chap in Ecouché, hauled out in front of a firing squad; I heard about that one.'

'You say it's as bad as it can get, but then they go one step further,' Marcel continued, in bitter tones. He glared at Albert. 'You haven't forgotten what happened over in Boucé?'

Silence stretched between them. Albert remembered, all too well. Odette was the one who brought the news, choking back sobs of rage and distress. 'How could they do that,' she cried out, 'how could they?'

A loud knock at the workshop door took them both by surprise. Marcel flattened himself against the wall and peered through the shop window. After a few moments he relaxed, stepping back.

'It's not the Boche.' He beckoned towards Albert. 'Who the hell is it, though?'

In the fading light, all Albert could make out was a man with a flat cap pulled low over his eyes, struggling to keep hold of a small boy. He peered again, stepped back with a groan. 'It's my mate Arnaud, he's got Nicolas in tow.'

The protesting child was dragged through the door the moment it was opened.

Arnaud was out of breath. 'Had to remove him from a compromising situation. At the Town Hall, he was, scrambling up onto a window ledge.' He shoved the boy towards Albert, exasperated. 'All we need, on a day like this, '

Albert grasped Nicolas by both shoulders, giving him a shake. 'I'll have your hide, you little. . .'

'It's not fair, Papa,' Nicolas protested, trying to squirm out of his father's grip. 'I was just trying to find out! The Boche are murdering someone in there, you should hear the shouting and screaming. . .'

'Listen to me, boy! Whatever goes on in there is no concern of yours. If you don't mind your own business you'll be getting yourself into trouble in a big way.' The young scamp deserved more than a good shake. 'Up to your room, and stay there.'

Nicolas skulked out, casting bitter glances at the adults before he slammed the door. Arnaud's face wore the glazed expression of someone who'd seen more than he could cope with. At a signal from Marcel, Albert produced the bottle of Calvados he kept on hand, pouring out a generous dollop.

Arnaud spluttered and choked for a moment, before he was able to speak.

'I've just been to the café, picked up the news from Pierre. He's better informed than that little terror of yours.' He drained his cup, set it aside. 'The Boche have put the screws on Bernard, trying everything to get him to confess it's a put up job.'

He pulled a crumpled handkerchief out of his pocket, wiped his brow. 'Pierre reckons they want to nail it on the FFL*, Bernard's little mishap gives them the perfect excuse. That bastard Kroger has threatened reprisals throughout the town – says he's got a list as long as his arm.'

'We know what that means,' Albert remarked, in foreboding tones, 'someone had better give them what they want, before they string us all up!'

Marcel was leaning into the workbench, kneading his fist into the pitted surface. Seemed to be taking the news hard.

'They've put an extra watch on the whole village,' Arnaud continued, 'reinforcements are already coming in, I've seen them . . Where are you off to?' Marcel was heading for the door.

'Thought I'd check up on the latest developments. I'll get back to you before curfew.'

# Bath Time

Steaming water splashed from the *bain-marie* into the bucket. She turned the tap off, emptied the bucket into the tin tub on the flagstone floor. Dipping her elbow into the water, she offered each cheek to the rising steam. Too hot for Claude, but it would cool down by the time they managed to get him in. She'd need to top it up for Thérèse and then again later on, if she could get hold of Nicolas. Albert would have to manage without this time.

The back of her throat tightened. What if. . . She could see the grey uniforms, the hard set faces rapping at the door, dragging her outside to dig a rifle into her chest, kicking her shins. She shuddered at the thought of what they might do to Thérèse, to both of them.

The sound of boots on the pavement outside drew her to her feet, heart pulsing in her throat. So many of them in the streets today, more than you'd expect on a Sunday evening. But then, this was no ordinary Sunday.

There would be news, it would take time to find out, she told herself, again. Albert would come back as soon as he could, to let them know.

She picked up the folded towel from the table and gave it a shake, draped it over the railing of the stove to warm up. The Boche could go ahead and murder them all in their beds, but Sunday night was bath night. She allowed herself a tortured smile. If they had to be dispatched, they might as well get themselves cleaned up for it.

Thérèse appeared in the doorway, eyes wide with apprehension. Claude whimpered and squirmed in her arms. 'Maman, will they. . .'

'Don't be ridiculous, my dear. Hold on tight, while I pull these clothes off him. You know what a fuss he makes about getting wet.'

'But Maman, Nadette told me. . .'

'You don't need to pay any attention to what she says or what any of them might tell you, Thérèse. We're just ordinary folk, hardly likely to be of interest to the Germans, it's a waste of time speculating about such things.' Seeing the stricken look on her daughter's face, her tone softened.

'The Germans can post up all sorts of threatening notices, *cherie*, but we don't need to get into a stew about everything we hear. If there is anything we need to do, your Papa will tell us soon enough. In the meantime, we should just get on with our lives as best we can. Don't you think that would be best?'

The protests of Claude put an end to her lecture. Lucette knew that the two of them would have their hands full until he was bathed and clothed. At least it would distract Thérèse, stop her fretting. Such wild rumours flying about: lists of hostages, deportations, the whole village to be torched. She shook her head. Claude was a welcome distraction for her as well.

She held out her arms for the little one, making a game of swinging him into the tub. 'Let's have a bit of a splash, *mignon*. Oops-y!'

Claude screamed, thrashing about until Thérèse dropped an apple into the water. Transfixed by the spinning yellow globe, he soon became absorbed in trying to capture it. Lucette pulled out the remnant of a *savonette** from her pocket. 'I've been saving this for a special occasion.' She worked up a lather in the palm of her hand. 'There should be plenty left when it's your turn.'

Thérèse glowed with admiration. 'Maman, you never cease to amaze me! How do you do it?'

Lucette gave a wry smile. 'It's an acquired skill, my dear.'

They were bundling Claude into a towel when a soft tap sounded at the kitchen door. Thérèse drew her breath in. Lucette remained utterly self-possessed, wiping her hands on her apron as she rose to her feet. The Germans would practically bash the door in, she knew that much.

'Don't worry, *cherie*, it must be someone we know, knocking like that. Keep him wrapped up, there's a draft coming in from the passage.'

Odette bustled into the room, breathless with excitement, her hair dishevelled, scarf trailing. 'They've changed their minds,' she announced, as soon as she could speak. 'We've had a close shave, though, I can tell you. The way they were tackling Bernard. . .'

Lucette placed a restraining hand on Odette's arm and turned towards Thérèse, smiling reassurance. 'You see, my dear, we didn't need to fret, nothing is going to happen to us. And now, could you please take him upstairs for me? He won't give us a moment's peace, otherwise. Get him ready for bed, everything is laid out.' Seeing her disappointed expression, she added, 'I promise I'll give you a full report later on.'

Left on their own, Odette sank into a chair. She cast an approving glance towards the steaming tub. 'You don't seem to have been in much of a panic round here. I've just come from Marie Perrauld. She had their bags packed, all set to do a runner.'

Lucette poured out a cup of chicory coffee, spilling some of it on the table. She hadn't noticed until then that her hands were shaking. She poured another one, taking more care.

'You'll have a cup, won't you, while you explain everything? We've heard such conflicting accounts, we don't know what to believe.'

Odette needed no further encouragement. 'I've had it direct from the horse's mouth, Pierre was at the town hall, as it happens, trying to repair the staircase. He could hear Kroger sounding off, hell bent on retaliation, he was, fired up even more when he couldn't get a yea or nay out of Bernard. Kroger decides that every house on Bernard's street must be hiding resistance supporters. He's going to smoke them out, he says, teach the rest of us a lesson; if the whole town burns down so much the better. He gets his minions to shove Bernard into a cell, then sends his dispatch officers out to drag in the gendarmes and summon his squadron from their billets.'

Odette paused to draw breath, drawing satisfaction from the impact of her words. 'Then, wouldn't you know, Madame Vampoule herself strolls into headquarters, for all the world like she owns the place. She's wearing some sort of hip hugging, low-cut number, where she got it from I can't imagine, haven't seen the like in this town since before the war, if that. She demands a private interview with Kroger, won't take no for an answer, tells every grey suit on the premises that she's got some vital information concerning the whole incident: if they knew what she knew they'd be letting her speak, and so on. They keep saying he's busy not available make an appointment, you know, the usual, but seeing as she's the notary's wife they couldn't really chuck her out, so she finally gets what she wants. After a half hour or so, Kroger pokes his head out the door and tells his officers to call it off. Then he slams the door shut.'

Odette folded her arms and leaned back in her chair, meeting Lucette's astonished gaze with a knowing look.

'Madame Vampoule didn't emerge from that office for quite a long time.'

Lucette sat down at last, overwhelmed by the turn of events. 'She's a brave woman, to risk speaking up,' she felt impelled to say, 'But could she really. . .'

Odette nodded, raising her eyebrows. 'Those are the sort of women with power these days.' She leaned towards Lucette. 'You know as well as I do what they've been saying about her and I hope it's not true, that rumour about her relationship with a certain person in the medical profession. Shocking, it is, for a married woman.'

Lucette coloured, casting her eyes down.

'Now the tables are turned, we're all licking her paws with

gratitude!' She heaved herself into an upright position. 'Times being what they are, we've got to put up with these things.'

'Have another cup,' Lucette offered, the conventions of hospitality providing a welcome distraction. 'It's very tempting, my dear, but I really must be going now. I still haven't been to see Clémence and I promised to let her know the latest as soon as I could.'She brushed her skirt down, firmly, glancing up to add, 'I knew there was something else. Your husband is at the café. He said he'll be home soon.'

Lucette offered a dry smile. 'I should have known. Thanks for passing the message on.'

Odette lumbered towards the door, shaking her head. 'Poor old Bernard! Probably didn't know what he was doing, he was so pissed. What a price to pay for a bit of nonsense!'

'What's going to happen to him?' Lucette asked, fearful of what she might hear.

Odette drew a forefinger across her throat. 'The day after tomorrow,' she said. 'Not sure about his wife, you'll have to ask Monsieur Griot.'

The door closed. Lucette leaned her head against it. Thérèse was calling. Drawing herself together, she took a deep breath, turned towards the stairs.

# A Country Walk

Crossing the footbridge that afternoon, she took the path along the river Senevières, skirting Madame Brionne's orchard, turning into the lane heading towards Montmerrei. The urge to remove herself as far as possible from the seething turmoil of the town square drove her on, hastened her steps. Most of her neighbours, driven by curiosity or fear, would be congregating there to witness the executions. An image of the guillotine flashed before her: prisoners on a tumbril wheeled through a gesticulating crowd, eager for heads to roll.

It won't happen like that, she told herself, severely. Albert could have explained the procedure, but she hadn't wanted to ask. He'd gone out to meet up with his friends at Odette's. They'd be there, watching: that much he'd told her.

Thérèse had insisted on remaining behind. 'I'll be fine, Maman, you mustn't worry, just go, get some fresh air,' she repeated, utterly intransigent. She would stay indoors, at the back of the house, as promised. Claude was asleep, Laurence due to arrive soon, what more could she do?

The gate to the Marivale farm was closed. From the other side, a collie ran towards her, barking furiously. No sign of Madame Marivale, she would have appeared on her doorstep if she'd been at home. It was only too likely she had found some excuse to go to town, the urge to witness such an event hard to resist.

Where was Marcel? Three days, now, since he received that long dreaded summons from the German authorities, those cold commands which even now had the power to hammer her heart.

'*Statutory Work Order*

*Marcel Guillaume Richaud*

*In accordance with the statutory decree of 16th February, 1943, you have been selected to go to work in Germany. You are requested to. . .'*

He'd been lucky to avoid the *Relève* all this time, Marcel reminded her. Rumours were rife, there were signs of resentment. 'How did he got away with it?' some folk were saying. According to Albert, Raymond Duval had told everyone that it was Marcel's duty to volunteer and if he didn't, they would all suffer the consequences. 'The law's the law, he should know that by now!'

When she tried to remonstrate with Marcel, he launched into his favourite expression of the moment : 'there is no glory in being French, there is only one glory; to be alive.[8,]

Raymond's son had been in the first *Relève*. She'd asked Madame Duval about him just the other day, the news hadn't been good. Digging trenches for subsistence wages on twelve hour shifts, slave labour was what it amounted to, she complained.

No one in their right minds would willingly go off to Germany these days, Marcel kept on saying. The Germans had stopped allowing conscripted workers to come home for visits, they were so desperate that conscripts would disappear, going into hiding, to avoid returning to Germany.

'Don't worry. I'll find a way to get round this,' Marcel insisted. If he could process a medical exemption certificate, similar to the one Laurence had been supplied with, his conscription would be postponed. The fatal incident provoked by Bernard, with all the associated upheaval, might result in a delay of several weeks. There would be more time to organise the paperwork, find some way around it. Menier was on his side.

At the top of the meadow, black and white cows formed a loose cluster alongside the hawthorn hedge. They turned their heads to track her progress up the sloping path, no doubt hoping she'd call them, milking time coming up soon. The more enterprising ones started plodding in her direction, giving up hope only when she was out of sight.

Hazelnut trees lined the far end of the next field, the pale green of new growth fringing the dark evergreens behind them. If all else failed, Marcel would go into hiding, supplementing the ranks of the *maquis*\* known to be inhabiting Écouves Forest. They'd never find him in such a vast wooded area. It wouldn't be such a terrible prospect for him. There were farms nearby, sympathetic country folk willing to help, a network he could draw upon for communication and support.

She stopped short, a sudden realisation draining the life blood from her. If he joined the *maquis* she wouldn't be able to see him. What a bitter twist of fate, this Occupation, drawing them together only to wrench them apart!

The path skirted round the edge of the trees, leading her uphill. It would all come to an end soon, Marcel had assured her. What would happen then? She tripped on a stone, steadied herself. Would they pick up the threads of their daily lives just as though the war had never happened? As though nothing had changed for any of them? It was impossible to imagine her existence, now, without Marcel. He was part of her breath, her life, his presence as essential as the bread she queued up for every day. It was as simple as that.

The rattle of a cart jolted her back to consciousness. She was crossing the field alongside the lane which led into Montmerrei, there was the church spire, peeking through the gaps in the beech hedge. She could hear the driver urging his horse along, eager to get home. Time she went home, too, it would take at least half an hour to walk back, she'd gone further than she'd intended.

The blackthorn alongside the path was covered in blossom. A crumpled bit of paper had come to rest there, impaled on one of the thorns. Someone must have dropped a discarded message on their way home, she could pick it up, at least. A curious impulse prompted her to smooth out the creases, trying to decipher the contents. It might be something important.

'On nests in the heather
In an echo of my childhood
I am writing your name…

She felt the heat rise to her cheeks. So intimate, the tone, she would have taken it for a love letter. But this was printed out on rough paper, just like a notice in the town hall. Who would want to do such a thing? She looked back towards the village, as if the familiar shapes of roof and spire could offer a solution. The cart was long gone. Not a soul in sight.

Retracing her steps as she continued on her way, she sounded out the lines in puzzled wonder.

'In the fields, on the horizon,
On the wings of birds
And on the mill of shadows
I am writing your name…'

It seemed to be some kind of poem, but without rhymes. She could remember learning some poetry at school; she'd liked the ones by Lamartine. The edges of the paper were intact, clearly this wasn't torn out of a book. *Tiens*! Another one, dangling from the briar arching over the path. She tugged it away to scan the contents, comparing the two tattered specimens. Exactly the same.

Paper was scarce these days, usually reserved for specific purposes. She read the opening lines again, her gaze registering a bewildered, almost aggrieved disapproval.

No point wasting time in speculation. Stuffing the papers into the pocket of her blouse, she set out on her way, hastening her steps. Claude would be up by now, Thérèse beginning to worry. She could hear the soft rustle of paper as she walked along. Her hand slid towards the pocket, as if magnetised. There might be a clue she'd missed, or even some sort of code.

'Schoolbooks…trees…golden images…warriors weapons…nests. . .heather'.

The insistent rhythm of the lines began to claim her, slowing her to an ambling pace.

'On health returning
On risk disappearing
On hope without memory
I write your name
And by the power of a word
I begin my life again
I was born to know you
To recognise you
Liberty'[9]

She pressed the papers to her chest, feeling the rush of tears rising, throat contracting. It was a good feeling, comforting, uplifting, the way she felt when she heard Thérèse singing as she swept through the house.

Beyond the next rise, she thought she could detect the silhouette of a lark, looping and surging across the leaden sky, winging its way towards the glow of crimson sun on the horizon. It came to her, then, what she was experiencing. Hope. She'd almost forgotten how it felt. Brushing her eyes with the back of a hand, she repeated the last few lines, a smile on her lips. Folding the bits of papers with care, she tucked them into her chemise. It was strangely comforting to feel the touch of the papers against her skin. She could hardly wait to show them to Marcel.

# A Stew

She was chopping cabbage with a vengeance, wielding a knife that looked as though it could sever a limb. A log tumbled from the basket Albert had just carried in, rolling across the flagstones. She looked up, frowning, knife poised, registered his presence with a brief nod as she resumed her task. He fumbled behind the stove until his hands made contact with the poker. The logs crackled as he dropped them into the stove.

At the back of the stove, the lid of a *marmite** rattled, contents bubbling. He gave an appreciative sniff as he stepped out of her way, his mouth watering, memories of his mother's beef stew conjured up. Francine never failed to put him on edge, but he had to admit, her cooking was the best he'd sampled in years. Certainly hadn't picked up the knack from her mother.

She wasn't wasting any time, either, that daughter of his. Back home for a week now and she'd already got hold of a good bit of brisket. Wouldn't do to ask her how she pulled that one off, not while she was in one of her moods. If she wanted to cultivate an extra friendly relationship with the butcher, that was her business. Just make the most of the change of menu, no questions asked; it might encourage her to stay for another couple of months. Paris was no place for a young woman these days, she must have worked that one out by now.

He set the poker against the wall, taking care not to let it slide. When he turned around he could see she'd finished off the cabbage and was hacking at some potatoes and turnips. Evidently dinner wouldn't be ready for some time yet. He was heading for the door when she spoke up.

'Excuse me, Papa, I'd like a word, if you could spare a moment.'

That voice had a cutting edge to it. He stopped dead, eyeing her with suspicion. '*Pardon?*'

'I said, I'd like to have a word, if you don't mind.'

What nonsense was the girl going to stir up now? Something about Nicolas? She was always the first to find out what he'd been up to, that little rogue. The fuss she made when he knotted all her handkerchiefs together so he could shimmy down from the bedroom window! She would have done the same, herself, at his age, of that he had no doubt.

Francine continued to chop vegetables as though she wanted to dispatch them. 'You might as well sit down, Papa,'she said, 'I've got to finish this lot off, no one else is going to do it for me.'

It couldn't be Nicolas she was worried about: the lad was staying with his Uncle Robert until the end of the month. Some new gripe about the neighbours, perhaps, or even Laurence? He'd noticed how that lad had kept a low profile ever since Francine's return. Hardly surprising, given the less than complimentary response from her when Thérèse announced their engagement.

He lowered himself into a chair with a sigh. If Francine was in one of her moods, it was more likely to be about her mother. The two of them had regular spats, for no reason at all as far as he could tell. No option but to hear her out.

A heap of green and yellow cascaded into the pot. Francine stirred vigorously, bashed the lid on.

'Without garlic it's not going to be up to much,' she pronounced, eyeing him with an incriminating stare. He cast his eyes down, remembering the fuss he'd created last time. Garlic! He'd never liked the stuff and never would.

She was wiping her hands on her apron, now. The chair creaked in protest as she fell into it. He groped in his pockets for his tobacco pouch and *briquet*, anything to postpone the moment when he'd be obliged to meet her eye. When he finally stole a glance, she seemed to be absorbed in polishing her nails. We can both play a waiting game, he told himself, as he crafted the perfect cigarette.

Francine stretched a hand out, fingers splayed, frowning at the results. Speech came at last, words falling, as if by chance. 'Your friend, Marcel. . .'

Albert froze, *briquet* in hand. She was rubbing a thumbnail with the corner of her apron.

'Rather unfortunate that he's managed to get off the latest *Relève*, under the circumstances.'

He set the *briquet* down. After a moment, he replaced the cigarette, folding the pouch with careful deliberation, taking pains to align it with the edge of the table.

What could she know about the nagging twinges of suspicion aroused by a sudden handshake, an excessively hearty greeting, an averted eye. He would stash those impressions away, ferret them out, later to chew them over, searching for excuses to be able to dismiss them out of hand. It seemed as though Marcel hadn't been the same person for the past few months, ever since those night shifts started up. Everything seemed strange, topsy-turvy, the normal routine completely skewed. Orders were a month behind, he wasn't used to such a state of affairs. For regulars, such as his friend Raymond, it didn't matter a jot, but some of his new clients might just take themselves elsewhere. What a time for Francine to decide to have a go at him.

He cleared his throat, remembered not to spit, swallowed hard. Best to tackle Francine head on. Don't give way, not for a moment.

'What do you mean? I thought it was rather enterprising of him, the way he managed to find a loophole in the system. Good old Menier, gave him a medical history to keep him off Compulsory Work Service till kingdom come!'

She was frowning at her other hand. 'Got your *Opinel* on you?' He watched her grip the pocketknife like a pen, levering it to scrape behind the thumbnail. Finally, she rubbed the blade on her apron and handed it back, remarking, 'I should have thought that you, especially, would be relieved to get him out of the way.'

He tried to fabricate the astonishment he wished he could feel. 'Marcel? What are you talking about? He makes himself very useful around here, I'd be sorry to see him go.'

Francine dropped her hand on the table, drumming the fingers. 'Useful! To whom, I wonder?' The tone was bitterly ironic.

He scraped his chair back. 'I don't know what you're talking about.' It might be better left unsaid, whatever she was going to tell him. 'Anyway, there's work to be done. I'll be . .'

She glared at him. 'Perhaps you'd rather hear it from someone else, that's fine with me.' She began to flick crumbs from the table.

Half out of his chair, he thumped down again, breathing hard, thoughts whirling. Sheer determination propelled a more successful attempt to rise. Pacing the room, he tried to reason with himself. If there really was something he ought to know, then no point leaving it at that. Better to pin her down, find out what she was insinuating before she gabbled some nonsense elsewhere. If it was anything to confirm his worst suspicions, he might as well find out. He stopped short, took a deep breath, heeling round to face her. There she was, at the stove again, chopping away as if she'd never left off.

'Come on then. Out with it.'

'All right, all right! Don't rush me,' she retorted, scraping parsley into a neat pile, contemplating the result. He heard a strangled attempt at a laugh. It came out sounding like the bark of a muzzled dog.

'Just a bit on the side, as they say,' she remarked, wiping her eyes with the back of her hand.

The well-worn excuse was balm to his ears, laughter blissfully contagious. 'Ha!' He could feel his jaw cracking into a wide grin. 'Is that all? That's no news to me! He's always had an eye for the ladies, Marcel. Not much I can do about that!'

His brow creased as his thoughts took an unexpected turn. Leaning back against the table, he folded his arms.

'Has he started chasing Thérèse in earnest, this time, now that Laurence is taking an interest in her? Wouldn't put it past him.' His eyes travelled up and down Francine's slim figure. 'You haven't been putting yourself out for him, have you?' He wouldn't have been surprised, the way she carried on, sometimes.

A potato flew past his ear, thudding on the wall behind. 'Steady on!' he protested.

'I don't know why I bother,' she announced, turning back to the *marmite*, stirring the contents with renewed vigour. The stew simmered like a volcano. He could hear his stomach rumbling in sympathy.

She spun round, brandishing a wooden spoon at him. 'Your friend Marcel is spending a lot of time here.' The spoon jabbed spokes in the air, punctuating her words. 'A lot of time alone with Maman.' She glared at him. 'Do I need to elaborate?'

Albert turned his back on her, driving clenched fists into the table. His head was spinning, memories ricocheted back and forth in his consciousness. All those evenings of *Belote*, Lucette sitting by the fire, setting her knitting aside to make cups of coffee for them. Had there been something else going on all along? Sweat trickled from his brow as the heat rose. When he asked Marcel to stay in the house, they must have been laughing. Such a good idea, it seemed, at the time; what a deluded fool he'd been, to encourage their nonsense!

He sat down again, elbows on the table, let his head drop into his hands. Francine was fiddling about with a heap of crockery on the sideboard, rearranging things to suit herself. He scowled, suddenly resentful. That girl was always looking out for trouble, what could she really know? Coming back from Paris with a head full of notions, when she saw Lucette and Marcel together, she'd put her own spin on things. That must be it. He stared at his feet, considering. Decision made, he let out a sigh of relief and stood to confront her.

'You've got it all wrong, girl. Marcel's been staying here to do us a favour.'

He heard her give a snort, but carried on, regardless, words pouring out in an effort to convince them both. 'You were still in Paris when I

95

was put on evening shifts at Surdon Junction. Just a couple of nights, it was, to begin with, but every time an incident occurred, the Huns tacked another night on. Your Maman was all on her own with little Claude, and Thérèse too young to be much use. Fretting with anxiety, she was, and what. . .'

'Tell me about it! I've had an earful of that nonsense from Thérèse. She's such a wimp she nearly pisses herself every time there's a knock at the door.'

'You heard about that woman in Argentan. . . '

'Stick to what's going on around here,' she cut in, turning round to confront him. A marble rolled off the sideboard, rattling along the flagstone floor.

'I'm telling you again, it would have been better for all of us if he'd gone off to do his stint in Germany,' Francine continued. 'Why should he be let off when so many others have had to go? Dodging the *Requis** and then helping himself to. . .' She shook her head, grabbed a cloth and started wiping the sideboard. 'You were just asking for trouble, you know. Bound to happen, the way it's been going.'

'*Salope!*' He was on his feet, grasping the sides of the table to stop himself lunging at her. 'You should watch your tongue, the way you come out with such nonsense, it just goes to show the sort of riff-raff you hang about with in Paris.' He flinched, standing his ground as a bowl shattered on the floor. Not so many years ago, he would have given her a hiding for less than that.

She was contemplating the broken shards with a puzzled frown, seemingly oblivious as to how they had got there. Leaning against the sideboard, she crossed her arms in resignation. 'Go ahead, pile up the insults if it makes you feel better, but you'd be better off listening to what I've got to tell you. Before you hear it from someone else.'

A heavy silence closed in around them. The clock in the hallway struck six. A dog howled in the lane. He braced his back against the bar of the stove, feeling the heat rise, his neck clammy with sweat. He couldn't move.

Francine ambled towards the table and stood there, poised, fingers strumming the pace of some new train of thought. When she spoke again, the tone was suffused with ironic insinuation.

'Cushy little job she's taken on, recently, isn't it?'

Albert started. What was the girl leading up to now?

'Yes, very convenient,' she continued, 'delivering telegrams for the post office in the afternoons. Baby Claude asleep, Thérèse keeping an

96

eye, Maman free to go off on her bicycle. Perfect little setup, isn't it? That friend of yours has it all worked out.'

She seemed to be waiting for him to respond. The next words were heavily charged, confidential, for all the world like an informer blowing the cover on some resistance operation.

'I've seen her, you know. I know where she goes when she's supposed to be delivering those 'telegrams.'

The words drove stakes into him. He gripped the bar of the stove, immobilised, unfocused eyes staring into space.

'They're never seen together,' he heard the relentless voice continue, 'oh no, he makes sure of that!' Francine was sitting on the edge of the table now. 'First of all, your friend follows a little path through the park, alongside the château. After a little while, Maman comes through the park gate, wheeling her bicycle. She's going in the same direction. Strange coincidence, isn't it?'

He shook his head, struggling against the weight of her evidence. 'Of course it's a coincidence. Two people happen to go for a walk in the park, that doesn't mean a thing.'

'If that's what you choose to think. Strange that it should have happened more than once, that's all.'

Albert was leaning into the wall. 'I can't believe it,' he murmured.

She was angry now as she drew herself up to confront him. 'If you think I'm deliberately trying to put down my own mother, you'd better think again! I tell you, she's being taken advantage of, deluded by that womaniser!'

She strode back to the stove, shoved the *marmite* to the far corner, tore her apron off. 'I've had my say, you can take it or leave it. I'll tell you one thing, though, I'm not going to stay here long enough to see what happens.' The door slammed shut behind her.

Albert drew himself up, stared blankly at the wall for a long time, a frown puckering his brow. He gave a deep sigh. Turning around, he began to shuffle towards the workshop.

# Tryst

He was urgent in his demands, as though pressed for time, taking her against the rough-timbered wall of the shed, finishing almost before she caught her breath. Then, full of remorse, he covered her breast and shoulders with kisses, begging her forgiveness. She buttoned her dress and smoothed it down, composing herself. 'It's all right,' she told him, 'please don't worry about it.'

She spread a blanket out on a bed of dried leaves and straw, settled herself down on it, waiting for him to come and sit beside her. He had opened the shed door and was surveying the clearing with wary eyes. He squatted down at last, picked up a twig at random, snapped it into bits with an abstracted air. He seemed to be pre-occupied with heavy thoughts. She'd learned to recognise that look, to ask no questions.

'Read to me,' she suggested, finally, fingers stroking his arm, tugging at his attention with the familiar ritual of their stolen afternoon trysts. Perhaps it would ease his anxiety, help him focus on the brief time they could share. Everything seemed strange today.

Marcel sighed, offering an apologetic smile. He pulled a slim volume from his pocket and leafed through well-thumbed pages, taking his time to make a selection. She settled back against the wall, relieved, expectant.

He'd been so excited that evening when she produced the scraps of paper she found on her walk. She would never forget that first time he read the poem, his voice an incantation to set her spine tingling. 'Liberty'. The words invoked so much for her, more than she could ever say.

A few days later he turned up with a booklet of poems, some written by the same person, others by someone called Aragon. The words sang, soaring into space like flocks of swallows. She could never hear enough of them.

Clearing his throat, Marcel began at last, a low monotone, gaining pace and volume as his voice found the measure of the lines.

'What else could we do, for the doors were guarded,
What else could we do, for they had imprisoned us,
What else could we do, for the streets were forbidden us. . .'

Bitter, harsh words, biting into her. She regarded him with dismay, scrutinizing his sullen features. Drawing her knees up, she cradled them in her arms.

'What else could we do, for she hungered and thirsted,
What else could we do, for we were defenceless. . .'[10]

The words died on his lips. He flung the book aside, pressed his head into clenched fists.

What was troubling him? She rested her palm on his arm, waiting until he took possession of it. He began to massage her fingers, his brow furrowed in thought.

He met her eyes, at last. 'Albert hasn't told you, has he?' The bleak gaze hollowed out her chest. Albert knows. She drew her hand from his, clapped it to her mouth in distress. They'd been so careful, all this time.

'What do you mean?' Her voice faltered. 'What has he said?'

The anxious tones seemed to penetrate his distracted consciousness. He drew her towards him, as if protecting her from a storm of denunciations.

'It's not what you think.' Gazing into her panic-stricken eyes, he stroked her arm. 'No accusations, no harsh words.' Her body softened.

'Let me tell you what happened, it's so unexpected, I'm still trying to absorb the shock.' He met her eyes for a moment, before resting his gaze on the view through the open doorway.

'I dropped by the workshop last night, on my way home from the printers; you know how Albert likes to have a chat at the end of the day. I wanted to check a couple of dates with him, seemed as good a time as any. He was sweeping the floor, hell for leather, the way he does, sometimes, when the mood takes him. "Let me give you a hand," I say, reaching out to take the broom from him, but he gives me such a look it stops me in my tracks. "I don't need your help," he says. I try to pass it off as a joke, telling him in that case I might as well see what I can do for his womenfolk. He stops sweeping, leans on his broom. "Suit yourself," he says, "but I'm telling you now, we won't be needing you to stop over any more."'

She felt her head spinning, blood draining from her limbs. 'He's still got night shifts,' she said, clinging to the last shred of an excuse, 'How does he expect me to . . .'

'I pointed this out to him. It doesn't seem the best time to abandon the schedule, especially with Francine still away. Albert shook his head, stubborn as ever. I wasn't going to argue, given the circumstances.'

She drew her knees up, collapsing into them. 'What are we going to do?' she moaned, sobbing, in spite of herself. She knew what he was going to say.

It was exactly what she expected and more. Neither of them could tell how much Albert really knew, but it seemed certain that he would be watching every move she made. 'It's not a good idea for you to be here even now,' he added, glancing at the door, 'but I had to see you, to talk to you. . .'

The problems and dilemmas of a compromised life began to storm her consciousness: Albert, his simmering anger, his bitter words of retaliation, the guilt which hounded her for the carnal sins she had committed, the children, their very innocence an accusation, Marcel, young, insouciant, free to go his own way whenever he wanted to. She pressed her fingers into throbbing temples, shoulders shaking.

His arm was around her, now, gently pulling her close. 'There now, *cherie*, easy does it. It's not the end of the world. Once we've booted the Germans out, we'll be able to make plans.'

She raised her head, a glimmer of hope kindling in her tear-struck face.

He lowered his voice. 'Don't ask me how or when, but I've got a feeling it will be soon. We'll be able to start again, you and I, making our future together. I'm sure we will.'

# 5 – 9 JUNE 1944

# Operation Overlord

He rapped softly, three light taps, followed by one, hard and firm. Count to three, then repeat, as necessary, he'd been told.

Peering into the murky depths of the neglected kitchen garden, he listened for the clomp of sentry boots in the lane nearby. All he could hear was the scuttling of some night creature in the shrubbery. The door was nudged just wide enough for communication. 'Overlord' he murmured. It gave way.

Inside, Robert clapped his shoulder in greeting, leading him through to the kitchen. A single candle flickered in a saucer on the table, casting long shadows over the group clustered around Menier's radio. The mellow strains of Charles Trenet filtered through a buzz of conversation.

André approached him, eagerly. 'Lucien, at last! We knew you'd show up. Ready for a bit of action? He rubbed his hands together. 'What a night it's going to be.'

Menier, in close conference with Henri, cast a sharp glance at them. 'Best not to speak too soon, we're still waiting for final confirmation.'

Robert was at his elbow now. 'That last message we picked up made about as much sense as a goose egg laid by a cow. "The long sobs of violins, of autumn"…Crafty work, that!'

Marcel chortled in spite of himself. 'A bit longwinded for a coded message, I thought at the time. Now I understand why. By the time those dim-witted Huns managed to decipher it, we'd already blown up the train at St. Loyer!'

Luke and Richard had both arrived by now, Richard still out of breath. 'Had to take a long way round to avoid a road block near Médavy.'

Trenet was finally winding down. 'The image of your lovely face melts away in the mists of time, in the mists of time.' Women's stuff, all that crooning, the lyrics were catchy, though, he had to admit. Every person in the room had fallen silent, turning, as if by one accord, towards the glowing box.

'This is London. The French speak to the French. Before we begin the next programme, please listen to some personal messages.' A buzz of static cut across the announcements, ripping into the few recognisable words coming through. Menier swore, thumped the case, switched the transmission on and off several times. Outbursts of indignant mutterings rippled through the assembled group. As if conjured away, the static disappeared, giving way to a droning intonation.

'. . . broken. I repeat. Eggs are fragile, like hearts, so easily broken. Second message. My heart is wounded, with languor, so monotonous. I repeat. My heart is wounded, with languor, so monotonous. Third message. Grey skies will clear. Grey skies will clear. . .'

'That's it.' In one brusque move, Menier switched off. He faced the group. 'You've just heard the coded message confirming everything we've been waiting for. Prepare yourselves, lads. Operation Overlord [11] will be underway within twenty-four hours.'

Marcel felt his body clench, pulse racing. A rising tide of excited murmurs swept through the room. André was gesticulating wildly, Robert elbowing Henri, who responded in kind. Richard looked stunned, perhaps he hadn't really expected anything to happen tonight, if indeed ever. Luke was the only one who seemed to remain composed. He wore a broad smile, nodding confirmation, as if already in the know.

Menier uttered a 'shush', raising his hand in warning until silence was restored. 'We've got to move fast and efficiently, finish the job before daylight. It's expected that the Germans will take the offensive soon.' He paused, gazing reprovingly at Robert and André until they fell silent. 'I can confirm that we'll be operating near Surdon Junction this time. The aim is to get rid of enough track to prevent movement of Boche troop reinforcements and equipment to the Front. The cell group at Ecouché will be undertaking a parallel manoeuvre. Is that understood?'

He waited for the full gamut of affirmative responses to subside. 'Now you've got the location, let's go over the procedures, make sure you're all on track.' They closed ranks, listening intently, as Menier began to elaborate.

# Missing

She couldn't understand why she was awake. Claude was sleeping peacefully, his fist tucked into his cheek. She listened for the usual sounds that might have disturbed her: the crow of a cockerel, neighbours stirring, thudding against the wall. Sometimes she'd wake up at dawn hearing Albert tramp into the kitchen, but there was no sound below. The noise came again, a repeated rumble echoing from some distant place. Was it thunder? It didn't really sound like a storm.

She slipped out of bed and groped her way towards the window. Parting the curtain, she could see lights flaring up on the horizon. The thud of a distant explosion reverberated in the night sky, firework flares heading for the full moon, falling back, peppering the horizon. She caught her breath. Surdon Junction was in that direction. Letting the curtain drop, she reached for a shawl, stumbled towards Marcel's room.

The door was gaping wide, the bedroom a black cavern, a forbidding reminder of his banishment. She sank down on the edge of the bed, running her hand back and forth across the tightly drawn covers, as if the cold caress could invoke his presence. Fear tightened its grip on her chest. What if Marcel and Albert were both in the same place?

There was nothing she could do. She fumbled back to her bed, burrowing under the covers, making an effort to stifle her worries, anxious thoughts revolving.

Towards dawn, she fell into an uneasy slumber, sleep punctured by the same irregular, detonated outbursts. In one of her broken dreams, Marcel and Albert were showing her around a large mansion, which somehow belonged to both of them. Albert took her hand, leading her up some stairs, opening doors into a succession of rooms. 'Look at this one,' he announced with pride, ushering her into a cold, empty room. Dead leaves drifted across the wooden planks of the floor, a dusty window was covered in cobwebs. 'All you need to do is to make up the fire,' he told her, in earnest tones, leaning closer, gripping her wrist. She pulled away, to find herself on a gravel path lined with beech trees. Hastening along it, she could see Marcel striding ahead, without a backwards glance. They came to the gate of a cemetery. Ancient tombstones struggled to remain upright in the engulfing vegetation. Marcel was beckoning, holding the gate open. 'It's this way,' he said, 'this is where we must go.'

'No', she cried, 'I'm not ready, no.' He was shaking his head, sadly, when she woke with a start. This time it was Claude, crying. Albert was still not home.

# The Return

'Isn't Papa coming down to eat with us?' Thérèse asked, nodding towards the empty place at the table. Lucette was sawing a loaf into quarters. She swallowed hard, trying to ease the lump in her throat. He'd never been this late before, not even that time they gave everyone an extra half shift as a punishment.

'Papa seems to have been delayed,' was all she could manage to come out with.

Thérèse besieged her with questions. Where could he be, never this late before, he would have told them, surely? What about Marcel, wasn't he supposed to be here when they were left of their own? 'Something must have happened to Papa,' she concluded, her voice quivering.

Lucette laid a restraining hand on her daughter's arm. 'Do calm down, Thérèse, let's not get into a panic, just when we've got Claude settled at the table.' She dipped a morsel of bread into a bowl of soup, letting him tug it from her hands. He sucked and chewed with relish. 'They must have been given a double shift and your Papa forgot to tell us,' she pronounced, as much for her benefit as for Thérèse. 'When you think about it, we've been quite fortunate that your Papa hasn't ever been this late before now. You know what they're like, his taskmasters, pigs, all of them.' She forced herself to swallow a spoonful. 'Come along, have your soup now, Thérèse, before it gets cold.'

Claude's cheeks were bulging with the bread he'd crammed in, but all his attention seemed to be focused on something he could see through the window. He crowed, stretching his arms out, legs pumping.

The door crashed open. Albert stood on the threshold. He didn't speak.

Thérèse gasped, clapped a hand over her mouth. Albert limped into the room, sank down onto a bench. His trousers were caked in mud, stained and streaked, a sleeve coming loose from a tattered jacket. He lifted the back of his hand to wipe streaks from his forehead, slumped against the wall, ignoring Claude's noisy attempts to attract his attention.

Lucette gathered the child into her arms, remonstrating. 'That's enough, *mignon*. Papa must be very tired now. Let's help him take his boots off, shall we?' Setting him down, she crouched beside Albert, focusing her mind on the practical task of undoing knots in the mud-caked laces. Thérèse poured hot water into a basin, casting anxious glances at the proceedings. Her eyes glistened with tears.

It was evening before Albert broke his silence. Settling Claude down for the night, Lucette caught glimpses of him through the bedroom window, watering the tomato plants, tending his tobacco seedlings, his usual activities after the family supper. When she came downstairs, he was standing in the middle of the kitchen, a bottle of Calvados in his hands. He examined the label, thoughtfully, as he sank onto a chair. Lucette handed him a glass, clearing a space on the table. She could hear the clatter of washing up in the scullery, Thérèse humming as she scrubbed.

Albert set the bottle down and took up the glass, turning it in his hands. 'I'm lucky to be here,' he announced, nodding his head, 'yes, lucky to be here, considering what went on last night.' Lucette stood stock still, pressing plates to her chest. A fork slid down, ringing on the flagstones.

The station at Argentan had been bombed, he told her. Explosives took a whole section of track at Surdon Junction. 'Practically under our noses,' he insisted. It was FFL* sabotage, he considered, without a doubt. Setting the glass down, he relapsed into a brooding silence.

Lucette could feel her heart pounding in her throat. Albert frowned, staring at the bottle on the table. As if suddenly recalling what it was for, he poured out a dollop of Calvados, twisting the bottle, from force of habit, a habitual quirk of his. 'Last night was the first time I've been caught up in the kind of situation I've been dreading.'

Concentrating hard, she carried the plates through to the scullery, returning to stand close by.

'You've got to do what you're told, no doubt about it, but when they expect you to betray your mates to them. . . ' the words trailed off.

The kitchen was closing in around her. She leaned against the sideboard, willing herself to breath in, to remain upright.

In a subdued voice, she asked, 'What do you mean, Albert?'

What had happened to Marcel was the question she dared not articulate. He must be injured, perhaps fatally injured, that's what Albert was going to say.

She made her way to the window, busied herself with drawing curtains, brushing the sill, anything to prevent Albert from observing her distress.

When she turned round, he was staring at the back of the door. Marcel's flat cap hung from a peg, waiting to be reclaimed. He met her eyes, opened his mouth as if about to speak.

'Maman!' Thérèse was coming through from the scullery, wiping her hands on her apron. She glanced at the drawn curtains, her face falling. 'Is it curfew already? Laurence said he'd come round after supper.'

Albert scraped his chair back, heaving a sigh, as he got to his feet. 'He'd better get his skates on. Less than an hour to go now . . .' The pulsing drone of aircraft thrummed, competing with his final words. Thérèse clutched at her mother's arm. The drone faded to a distant echo. Albert stepped through the kitchen doorway, stopping on the threshold to listen intently, surveying the sky. After a few minutes, he came back, closing the door firmly behind him. 'It's not coming this way.' He drew the bolt across, adding, 'I doubt you'll be seeing Laurence tonight.'

# The Morning After

The sky was a weight of thick grey cloud the next morning, the deep boom of distant explosions sounding with enough frequency to keep them indoors. Nothing seemed to fall close by, but they knew it would have been tempting fate to venture outside.

During the afternoon, the sounds of battle seemed to ease off, then stop altogether. Lucette couldn't bear to wait any longer. If she could only manage to speak to Odette, she might pick up news of Marcel.

Making her way down the Grande Rue, she was surprised to find so many shops open for business as usual, despite the recent bombardments. A straggling queue tailed into the street outside the grocers, neighbours exchanging comments, clutching their ration tickets as though it was a day like any other. The boulangerie was doing a roaring trade, selling the bread no one had managed to purchase that morning.

In the Place Centrale, an open-topped lorry, piled high with crates, bumped slowly across the square in her direction. German soldiers were crammed into the front seats, two more hung from the back, gesticulating wildly.

Odette was standing outside the café, a dust cloth in her hand. She waved at the passing soldiers, her smeared smile relaxing into a smirk as the vehicle turned into the Grande Rue. 'No front line for them. They've got the job of shifting all their plunder out of the château.' Sizing up Lucette's blank expression, she added, 'just in case the Allies get here and requisition the stuff. She chuckled. 'It wouldn't do to have their best Calvados fall into the wrong hands, now, would it?'

'Does that mean they're all going, then?' Lucette asked, in stunned surprise.

'No such luck, my dear. They're just, shall we say, spreading their assets, for the time being. Most of them will sit tight as they can, don't you worry.' She cast a wary look in both directions, drawing close. 'I was on my way to see you, actually. Menier asked if you could drop by at the surgery.' She lowered her voice. 'He's got a message for you.'

Lucette felt the blood draining from her limbs. 'You don't mean …'

Odette drew back. 'Not for me to say.' Casting a reproving look at Lucette, she registered the drawn face, the dark circles under her eyes, the distraught expression. With a forbearing shake of the head, she gathered Lucette's hands into her own, gently squeezing them. 'Don't worry! It can't be as bad as all that.'

Lucette was dimly aware of the inanimate body she seemed to occupy from that moment. It moved in the direction of the doctor's house, knocking hard on the oak door, sinking onto the threshold. Cold stone soaked into brittle bones, an eternity of waiting, until firm hands pulled her to her feet.

Menier was urging her to step into the house, steering her towards the kitchen. He pulled up a chair, guided her into it, poured out a glass of water.

'You must be relieved to be reunited with your husband,' he said, ' after such a night.'

She offered a blank stare, her brow puckering. Reunited with Albert? Relief? Was this what she was supposed to be feeling? She managed a tentative nod, mumbling something affirmative.

The doctor was gazing at her with an air of serious concern: she must be looking her worst. He urged her to drink, again, taking a seat close by.

'I've been dealing with several casualties connected with the incident near Surdon Junction.' She was all attention now, her eyes riveted on his face. 'Marcel Richaud is one you'd want to know about,' he continued, scrutinising her features as he spoke. 'A close friend of your husband's, isn't he?'

She cried out, immediately clapping a hand over her mouth. The room began to spin. Opening her eyes, she found herself collapsed in the chair, the doctor holding a cup to her lips. It wasn't water. She uttered a sob, liquid fire rolled down her throat. Spluttering, she pushed his hand away.

Menier was trying to tell her something, words flowing over her head. Finally she understood. Marcel was going to be all right, he was going to recover, she was not to worry. Warmth flooded her limbs. She gazed at the hands in her lap, they were hers again, she lifted her arm, it was tingling with renewed energy.

'Where is he?' she demanded, making an effort to sit up.

They'd found a safe place for him at the Marivale farm, the doctor explained. Marcel would need to remain hidden because of what had happened last night. It was better for her if she didn't know the details, best not to say anything, even to Albert. He waited for her to confirm that she understood.

'Madame Griot,' he continued, 'I need your help. Could I ask you to go and see Marcel's mother? It wouldn't do for me to be seen at the

Richaud house, there might be repercussions. Tell her that Marcel is safe, but don't reveal his whereabouts, whatever you do. We can't have her rushing over to the Marivale farm. Would you be able to do this for me?'

She was more than willing. Marcel was alive, he was going to be well, again, what more could she ask.

'It would be best if you could go as soon as possible.'

She nodded, struggled to her feet. If she hurried, there'd be time to get there and back before curfew.

'One more thing,' Menier added, a restraining hand on her arm. 'If I need to send a message through to Marcel, can I rely on you?'

She met his eyes. 'Of course.' Her voice quavered. 'Any time at all.'

# In Hiding

He shifted uncomfortably, wincing as he groped for the edge of the blanket, pulling it up over his bandaged leg, sinking back with a sigh of resignation into the bundled hay. There'd been plenty of time to come to terms with his surroundings. A ventilation grid filtered a flickering spectre of light over the stacked boxes and barrels, highlighting fragments of dusty farm equipment heaped in corners. He'd identified the pungent odour of cured ham and over-ripe apples, tracing it to the bundles hanging from the ceiling and the overflowing crates ranged along the wall. Behind these he could just see the edge of a box they must have heaved into place a few weeks ago, adding to the stash of emergency supplies for the next operation.

Overhead, the muffled thud of footsteps resonated through layers of floorboard. He was beginning to read the hours passing by the frequency of vibrations, the quality of light filtering through the edges of the trapdoor and ventilation grid, voices echoing through cracks in floorboards, cavities in walls. It must be daytime, perhaps even afternoon.

It shouldn't have happened, he kept telling himself, aimlessly plucking at strands of hay. Why couldn't they have been more vigilant, less foolhardy? The events of that night revolved in his mind like a recurrent reproach: the hours of undercover vigil in the woods, the gleam of railway track marking their destination, finally, the long awaited signal for action, the rehearsed, co-ordinated movements of the group. There was the inevitable false step, Henri's clumsy manoeuvre setting his teeth on edge. The throat-gripping tension of that last positioning of explosives in the ballast, wary foot-stepping to dodge the track as they ran for cover. Then shouts, gunfire, too close, too soon, the searing pain ravaging his leg. A last glimpse of the detonating flare of the explosion as he limped, staggered, fell. Hands dragged him further into the woods, where someone must have bound something round his leg. He sank into a pulsating well of darkness ridged with pain, until he became conscious of the firm touch of the doctor bandaging him up, waving the bullet at him like a charm, cracking a joke. 'Watch where you're going next time, you wouldn't want to offer one of these little buggers a home in the wrong place.' Monsieur Marivale was propping him up, his wife huffing and puffing up and down the stairs.

He twisted the corner of his lip into a wry smile. Not much rationing going on in the Marivale household. Madame was a marvel of a cook, eager to take the opportunity to make the most of her skills. The bowls of thick soup, casseroles, omelettes were the best he'd tasted in years. Still, they could serve him up a meal fit for old Boney himself and he'd turn it down for a bowl of sorrel soup and a sit down in his mother's kitchen, a crust of bread and an ersatz coffee with Lucette. He shifted position, unable to make himself comfortable, as anxiety took hold again. Had anyone thought to tell her?

The tread of feet overhead, indistinct voices. He rummaged beneath the blanket for his pistol. After a long moment his grip relaxed and he slipped it back into place. The Boche would have been shouting, tearing the house apart if they'd come looking for him. It must be the doctor, dropping by on his rounds, Madame Marivale doing the honours with obsequious pride. She made the most of his rare visits.

He heard the grating rasp of the bolt shifting on the trapdoor, the sudden clink as it gave way. Light streamed through the square gap in the roof. A head, no, two heads appeared, silhouetted against the brightness, Madame Marivale holding forth at her usual pace.

'And you'd never have guessed it was here, would you? I must say it's the perfect place, the way we've set it up; we've been able to hide quite a bit of produce even with the Boche sniffing around everywhere else, we thought the game was up last time they came, but they only looked in the big cellar under the kitchen, never imagined there'd be a separate cave under the dining room. Mind you, he's done a good job of concealing it, hasn't he, though I don't like to boast about my husband, at least, not when he can hear me, you know what men are like. Careful now, mind you don't slip on that ladder, it's getting wobbly with all the comings and goings we've had here recently, just hold onto that rope to guide you down, there, that's it. Now if you're sure you can manage, I'll get on with the supper, you just take your time, my dear.'

A cautious tread of feet descending, the swish of skirts, the scent of lavender. He felt his heart lift, warmth spreading through him as he leaned up on one elbow. She crouched down, setting her basket aside, taking his hand. Her lips touched his forehead, her smile was balm.

'I've brought a prescription for you.'

# JULY 1944

# Swimming

She was standing by the edge of the lake, fingers aimlessly twisting the straps of the faded blue swimming costume. Frogs croaked, hidden in the reeds and pondweed at the water's edge. Through gaps in the trees, the glint of high windows in the Château de Sassy, gleaming flickers in the afternoon sun.

Over on the far side, Nadette and Jeanine splashed and spluttered, engaged in a tug of war with a drifting branch. Jeanine made a lunge for it, taking possession. She caught sight of Thérèse, waved frantically.

'Come on, skinny shanks. It's not cold at all once you get used to it.'

'Hurry up!' Nadette spluttered, her voice ringing across the water. 'Jeanine's a right Hun, I tell you. Come and help me sort her out.' She grasped the other end of the branch, tugging at it with relentless determination.

Thérèse dipped her toes in, shivering, clutched her arms to her chest. She inched her way into the water, edging round a cluster of rocks barring her way. Mud sucked her feet into the depths, oozed between her toes. Pond weed brushed across her legs, twined round her ankles, a fish slid across her calf.

The water lapped at her knees. Better to plunge in now, get beyond the murk and mire of the lakeside. It wasn't such an effort after what she'd been through, just to get out of the house. If only she could obliterate the image of Maman's stricken, desolate face, that last glimpse before the door closed.

Fragments of reproaches ran circles round her head: 'too early in the season, too late in the day, they'd miss curfew, what about the regulations, it must be forbidden, there might be planes, bombs, tanks, what about the Huns lurking in the woods or the *maquis*, they might be just as bad, why did she want to swim anyway, so self-indulgent, with all the mending piling up in the basket and the ironing still to do.

She took a deep breath, letting it out slowly. She should make allowances, Maman must have been so upset, that day when Papa came home all cuts and bruises; yet she seemed calm and collected, as if that sort of thing happened all the time. Since then, she hadn't been quite her normal self, and who could blame her?

The water was thigh level now, seeping into her swimming costume. Papa would have thrown himself in long since, dragging her after him. He was such a good swimmer, pity he couldn't spare the time these

115

days.

A wave of compunction coursed through her: such an upheaval she'd left behind, for all she knew they were still arguing. Poor Maman, she'll give way just to put an end to Papa's ranting. He means it for the best, but even so. . . Just as well Francine wasn't around to add her own two sous worth.

She whisked some flecks of water onto her goose-fleshed arms. No point in worrying, best to make the most of her freedom, there'd be time enough to apologise to Maman later on. Taking a deep breath, she splashed out, gasping as the cold water slashed a sword through her chest. After the initial shock she was able to let the water take her, unresisting, swimming across to her friends.

The late afternoon sun was brushing the treetops by the time they emerged. There was a sheltered niche on the bank where they could make the most of the lingering glow of sunlight and warmth. It was time for an exchange of anecdotes, secrets divulged in whispered confessions, fits of hilarious giggling. During a lull in the conversation, Jeanine rolled onto her side, cupping her head in her hand to scrutinise Thérèse. A slur of a smile insinuated itself across her face.

'I've got some very interesting news, Nadette.' Thérèse darted a suspicious glance at Jeanine, then fixed her gaze on a clump of couch grass fringing her towel. Jeanine knew how to make her friends uncomfortable, Nadette was totally in thrall. 'A little bird told me some time ago that there's a certain young man Thérèse has been seeing quite a lot of.'

'Ooh,' crowed Nadette, rolling over to lean up against Jeanine. 'The virginal Thérèse! Tell us more, you spellbinder, go on.'

Thérèse sat up, murmuring protests, shaking her head with a nervous laugh. She pulled her damp towel around her, eyes trained on the darkening water.

'Come on, Thérèse, you can tell us, we'll find out soon enough anyway. It's one of the Richaud boys, isn't it?' said Jeanine.

It was more of a statement than a question, the way she announced it. Thérèse rubbed her ankles, flexing her feet, wriggling her toes. She peeled off a fragment of pondweed glued to her instep. Jeanine was relentless.

'I wonder which one, though? It could be the older one, Marcel, isn't that what he's called?' She raised quizzical eyebrows at Nadette, before fixing her gaze on her victim once more.

Thérèse started, the vehement denial sticking in her throat. With

Marcel around the house during the past few months, they were bound to put two and two together, coming to the wrong conclusions. She flushed with indignation, launching into explanations, cringing, inwardly, all the while, full of resentment towards Marcel, her parents, the situation she'd been drawn into. She pulled herself up, keeping her gaze fixed on the branch they'd dragged to the waterline. Why should she care what Jeanine and Nadette said about her?

Jeanine kept her in view, a sceptical smile curling her lip. And now Nadette chimed in, eager to make a fresh contribution. 'He seems to have developed an interesting limp recently, I must say. But how romantic, if it was all in your defence!'

Thérèse gave a shrug. 'Nothing so exciting. I heard tell that he tripped over a rabbit snare in the dark. Most unfortunate,' she added, in sanctimonious tones, pressing her lips together. The alder trees across the lake cast shimmering reflections, fading into distant pools of darkness. Thinking about Marcel gave her a hollow sensation in the pit of her stomach. She didn't want to understand why.

Jeanine's insinuating voice probed further. 'Yes, very unfortunate. Anyway, I think I must have been mistaken. It's the younger one, the dishy one that Thérèse has actually been going about with.'

'You mean Laurence?' Nadette demanded, incredulous. 'Thérèse, you lucky thing, I'm so jealous! Thérèse lowered her burning face while Nadette carried on, oblivious. 'Simone and I saw him passing by while we were in the queue for the boulangerie. He was strolling along, trying not to notice we were giving him the eye. So *appetissant* he is, slim and svelte, with those dark eyes! The way he smiles, it makes me tingle all over.' She grabbed a fragment of dried fern and started tickling the back of Jeanine's neck.

Jeanine shrugged her off, abruptly, her concentration still on Thérèse. 'All these close family connections,' she continued, in a suggestive tone, 'it's rather unusual, isn't it?'

'Is little Tessa playing a two-timing game?' Nadette teased. There were peals of laughter as Thérèse shook her head in indignation, pulling her towel round her shoulders. Nadette reached across to pat her knee. 'Don't get into a huff, Thérèse, we're only having a laugh. We don't mean it, really.'

'That's all right, then.' She forced a smile, shedding her towel as she sprang to her feet. Fragments of dead bracken clung to her legs. She brushed them off, stepped towards the water's edge.

Jeanine watched her. 'Well, I'd say it's all very interesting. But at least she can take her pick. They've both managed to escape the *Relève*, somehow or other.'

'We'll be able to toss a coin for the spare one, Jeanine!' The two girls dissolved into fits of giggling as Thérèse began to wade into the lake.

'Just going for one last dip,' she said, determined to maintain an air of indifference. 'Anyone coming?' Before they could respond either way she was off, slipping into the water with the compulsion of an otter.

The sun was low behind the trees, nearly time for curfew. They called out for her, repeatedly, before she emerged to join them.

# Struck Down

Where was everyone? The kitchen was as dim and deserted as a bar after closing time, curtains half drawn against a leaden sky. It had been raining most of the day. He'd been looking forward to the bustle and warmth, the smell of hot starched cotton, Lucette ironing at full spate, throwing comments over her shoulder: what on earth could she make for supper, could it be stretched, would Albert put up with it? Thérèse, folding and stacking the freshly ironed shirts, would glance up in surprise. Sometimes she'd arrive after he got there, coming through the back door after feeding the hens, to stop in her tracks. Her smile would sing to him.

Laurence stood with his offering in his hand, shoulders drooping. He'd looked forward to handing over the newspaper wrapped packet in an off-hand manner, watching Lucette unfold it with restrained anticipation. Her face would light up as the contents were revealed; she'd sniff with approval at the chunk of bacon. Thérèse would squeeze his hand with a caressing glance of admiring appreciation, while Lucette's eulogies rolled over his head. He'd swapped a whole bottle of Calvados for that bit of ham. Casting a proprietorial glance at the packet, he wondered whether to keep it for another visit, resisting the impulse to pocket his booty. They were bound to turn up soon.

He turned towards the stove, then stopped in sudden confusion. A young woman was stretched out in Lucette's armchair, watching him. Bare feet crossed at the ankle, resting on the bar of the stove, long legs, shadow muted, hands clasped behind her head. She wore a man's work shirt, half unbuttoned over an insubstantial dress. He cast his eyes down, took a step back.

'Sorry to disturb you. I was hoping to find Thérèse.'

Shifting uncomfortably, he could feel her gaze appraising him, as if considering whether to bother to reply.

'Thérèse is ill in bed. She's caught a chill.' The guttural tones seemed to challenge his presence, hitting hard with ill tidings. She swung her legs down, sprang to her feet, turning towards him.

'I'm s. . .s. . .so sorry to hear it,' he stammered, lifting his eyes, taking in her features in dazed recognition. An electric shimmer of blonde hair snaked round her shoulders, dark, narrow eyes pinned him down. Melting lips, crimson flares in the dim light. There was a faint imprint of Thérèse in her features, or was it something to do with the tilt

119

of the nose? Any resemblance was fading fast in the brash reality of living flesh.

She leaned against the bar of the stove, regarding him with bemused curiosity. 'Don't worry, it's all under control, at least, for the time being.' She glanced at the door, tapping her fingers.

He mumbled a few words in response, scratched his neck, wincing uncomfortably, rested his gaze on the wall, then the floor. He was longing to ask for details, but couldn't summon up the courage. It seemed that the subject was closed.

An image he'd tried to set aside flashed into consciousness: Francine, leaning from the bedroom window, taunting German soldiers as they passed by, her dressing gown all but falling off her. Rumour had it that she had slept with more than one of them, that she'd seduced the son of the pharmacist and gone to Paris to escape the consequences.

'It's been a long time, Laurence.' She was surveying him again, fingers twisting loose strands of hair. Her eyes travelled down to his feet and up again, making him aware of the bulge straining at his trousers. He forced himself to conjure up an image of Thérèse, her fingers brushing his cheek, her shy smile as he took her hand. It didn't help. Shifting his weight from one foot to another, his eyes were held captive by the living presence of Francine, the rise and fall of her breath, the soft cleft between her breasts. He found himself moving inexorably towards the stove as if drawn by a taut rope.

A door crashed open, sending a jolting tremor down his spine. Albert stomped across the room, offering a curt, unsurprised greeting to Laurence, immediately turning towards Francine.

'I couldn't get hold of Doctor Menier, they tell me he's had to go to Argentan. The Boche have ordered him to the bedside of a couple of officers there, no telling when he'll be back. He's bound to be too late, in any case.'

Francine took Albert's baffled cynicism as an act of provocation. She clicked her tongue, crossing her arms to confront him. 'What are we supposed to do, just sit here and wait?'

Impassive, he poured himself a glass of water. 'I'm going over to Sées to have a word with Doctor Bertrand. He might be persuaded to make a visit, given the circumstances.'

Francine began to raise objections: Doctor Bertrand was a doddering old fool, barely fit to take anyone's pulse, let alone deal with a crisis. They should wait for Menier, look after her as best they could, she knew what to do.

Albert drained the glass, slamming it down. 'I've made up my mind, let's have no more arguments.'

Francine shrugged, turning her back as Albert hurried out, leaving the door ajar. A dog howled in the yard. Francine kicked the door shut, deep in thought. Coming back into the room, she seemed surprised to find Laurence still there. His face was a chalk white smudge in the shadows, eyes wide with distress.

'You must tell me what happened,' he begged, 'Tell me everything. Please.'

Francine heaved a weary sigh, checked the supply of coffee in the enamel pot, shoving it towards the centre of the stove. She leaned against the cross bar, methodically doing up the remaining buttons of her shirt.

'A couple of days ago, Thérèse went for a little swim with her friends, over in the lake by the château.'

Laurence nodded, 'nothing unusual, she loves swimming.'

Francine's voice took on the bitter rant of a frustrated older sister. 'I know, I know, but under the circumstances, it wasn't a good idea. She's not been very well lately, coughing more than usual. Can't take any chances with a fragile constitution like hers.'

She reached for the poker, opened the stove door and started rattling the grate. '*Merde*! Nearly gone out. I need some wood.'

Laurence hastened to replenish the log basket, the pragmatic task would help to ease his anxiety. The fire revived, he found himself posing the questions he'd been longing to ask from the start.

It was the lungs, she told him, the chill had settled into her lungs. Pleurisy it might be or perhaps something worse. 'No point fussing until we know. Maman got herself into such a state, she's become worse than useless. Had to force some Calvados down her, put her to bed too.' She lifted the lid of the coffee pot, wrinkled her nose, shoved it aside.

'The shambles this place was in when I got here!' She waved a cup at him. 'No meals cooked for days, baby Claude wailing non-stop. Papa expects me to become some kind of angel in the house, while Maman mopes around crying and mumbling prayers into her handkerchief. What a family!' She poured coffee into the cup, shoved the pot in his direction with an enquiring glance.

Laurence shook his head, uttering a string of banalities in an attempt to express his concern, wondering, at the same time, when he'd be able to make his escape. His brain was whirling with conflicting emotions.

Clearing his throat, he said, 'I've got to go now.'

Francine had settled into Lucette's chair again, repositioning her feet on the cross bar. She barely glanced at him.

'Shut the door on your way out,' she called.

# 11 – 13 AUGUST 1944

# Liberation

Through a gap in the drawn curtains, a glimmer of late afternoon sun cast a diffuse glow over the sickbed, flickering across the face of the sleeper dozing in an armchair. Lucette stirred, rubbing her eyes with a yawn, taking in the darkened room as if for the first time. Casting an anxious glance at the inert figure pressed into the bed, she subsided back into the armchair, closing her eyes. Part of her consciousness was still in her dream, the cries of the market vendors surrounding her as she tried to choose between a golden, maize-fed chicken and a couple of plump, mouth-watering partridges. Marcel was brandishing one in each hand, smiling his approval.

She woke to the sound of a clattering thud. Her scissors lay on the floor next to the upturned sewing basket; half-darned socks and remnants of wool were scattered about her. Struggling to collect the bits and pieces together, she heard voices from the street calling out. It wasn't a dream this time. She could distinguish the hollow clopping of wooden sabots, the thudding pound of boots on a sun-baked road.

'They're coming, they're coming!' came the voice. Her grip on the sewing basket tightened. Thérèse was awake now, staring through the drawn curtains as if transfixed by the invisible activity unfolding in the street. In the next instant the door burst open, propelling Albert into the room, breathless, excited.

'It's today! At last! Second Armoured Division,[12] they're coming up through the forest road, heading this way. Leclerc's lads have done it: kicked the Boche out of Le Mans and Sées, we'll see them here before you know it!'

He strode towards the window, yanked the curtains aside, fumbled to release the shutters, cursing, as the hinge swung out unexpectedly, pinching his fingers. A wave of dusty heat poured into the room. He spun round to address Lucette and Thérèse, fizzing with excitement. Lucette recoiled, dumbfounded; she'd never witnessed such a degree of animation in him.

'You should see what's happening down in the square, Kroger's minions scampering round like headless chickens, back and forth from the chateau to the Mairie they go, shouting orders, loading up lorries, blowing whistles, trying to make themselves scarce before they're routed. We're going to see Leclerc and his men marching into town before you know it.' Before she could respond he was back at the

124

window, leaning out.

Noise and heat continued to spill into the room, invading her domain. Lucette kept a wary eye on Albert as she made her way towards the sick bed. She pulled the sheets up around the startled girl, stroking her head as she tried to focus on the turn of events. Were the Germans really on their way out this time? Surely not without a recurrence of the sort of incidents they'd been through in June? She flinched as she remembered the night when Albert failed to come home, that dreadful night when she feared for his survival, for Marcel's life.

There had been a steady trickle of conflicting reports since then, but once the crisis was over she had stopped paying much attention. It was all happening far away, up near the coast. Nothing had changed around here, except for more rigid curfew hours. German troops were still in the shops, in the streets, not smiling now, keeping to themselves more than ever before.

Thérèse pulled her sleeve, speaking in hoarse undertones. 'What's happening, Maman? Please tell me.'

'There's nothing to worry about, *chérie*. If Papa is right, the Germans will be leaving us. Perhaps they have already gone. Some of our own armed forces will be coming through the town. Everyone's excited, of course, but there's no need to let that disturb us.'

Time for her next dose of medication. Lucette cast a disapproving glance at the bottle of champagne on the side table, so out of place in a sickroom. It wasn't for her to challenge a doctor's prescription, Doctor Bertrand must have known what he was doing, though he did seem somewhat off-hand, rather dismissive in his manner. If only Doctor Menier would come back from Argentan, he could give Thérèse a proper examination, offer something more effective to help her. He would know just what to do.

She poured out half a foaming glassful. If the Allies were really on their way, the doctor would be able to return very soon. The Germans wouldn't be able to detain him, not any longer.

She sat beside Thérèse, carefully offering her a sip at a time. At least there was no shortage of the stuff. It still made her uncomfortable, thinking how they came by it. That night, just a few weeks ago, when Albert and Laurence burst through the kitchen door, trundling a wheelbarrow piled high with bottles, tins of ham, foie gras, sausages, and more. The pair of them covered in cuts and bruises, reeking of Calvados.

Just a friendly visit to the granaries of the château, they told her;

125

everyone knew it was where the Germans had been hoarding their supplies. 'We're only taking back what's ours by right,' Laurence declared, 'its all requisitioned goods from the farms and vineyards of our own countrymen.' She pursed her lips, frowning. It didn't seem right, just helping themselves like that.

Thérèse coughed, turning her head away. Lucette set the glass aside, hastening to ease her discomfort. The end of the Occupation, she reminded herself, as she pulled up the covers to settle her patient. She thought of the daily queue at the boulangerie, where they waited their turn, day after day, more often than not to witness German soldiers strolling in to buy up the last few loaves.

As she mulled over the implications of Albert's claim, she clicked her tongue in frustration. Where was the housekeeping money to come from now? What about Heinrich, Hermann, Adolf, Wilhelm, the armloads of washing they brought her, the ironing she did for them? She'd begun to take them for granted, the Germans in the streets and shops, the polite but insistent tapping, when they came to her door. It sometimes seemed as though the German soldiers and her fellow countrymen were all in it together, trying to get on with their lives as best they could: orders posted up, requisitions collected, men going off for Compulsory Work Service. Her hands dropped to her sides.

Liberation. That word invested with such hope, such anticipation, slipping into conversations, circling round expectant faces, ever since those terrible events in June. The poem she found in the field, was this all it meant? She tried to summon up the appropriate response. Relief, it must be, should be; joy, it could be, was not.

Turning away from the sickbed, she pressed her palms into her cheeks. Marcel. What would happen to them? She felt the familiar dull throb of pain circling her temples. Did she still want to see him? Those fugitive meetings and late night encounters seemed to have taken place in another era, the world which existed before Thérèse lay down in her bed and didn't get up again.

She sank back into her chair, closing her eyes. Liberation? The end of the Occupation? Let them stay, let them go, it made no difference to her. This room was her whole world now, the frail form in the bed her sole, enveloping concern.

The dust was beginning to tickle her nose, it made her want to sneeze. When would she be able to close the window? Albert was entirely absorbed in the events of the street, his bulky torso folded over the window ledge, a dark mass against the glaring sunlight. If she could draw the curtains shut on one side, it might keep the dust at bay. She made a cautious approach.

Her husband was waving windmill arms at a passer-by. 'Pierre! What's the latest?'

'The Yanks are coming full steam ahead,' Pierre shouted, 'you'll see them any minute now. Massive convoy trucks, wacking great Shermans, loads of troops, no wonder the Boche are making themselves scarce. The Allies took over Sées early this morning; this lot must be heading for Argentan, ready to flush the Huns out of another nest.'

'We don't want a bunch of Yanks here, what about Leclerc? Are you sure it's not his troops coming through?'

Pierre shrugged, spread his arms. 'No idea mate. Maybe he's sending this lot in to clear the decks for him.'

Raymond appeared at Pierre's shoulder. 'Leclerc's too busy rooting out the Panzers from the forest to bother with the likes of us. Let him get on with it; the Boche are getting out, that's the main thing.'

'Hurry up you two, you'll miss all the action,' someone called out, as she pulled a curtain across. Time to retreat to her armchair. She took up her workbasket, extracted a sock to darn.

Albert moved towards the door, evidently tempted to join his friends, only to change his mind. He must have decided that the view was better from upstairs. Curtains billowed round, he yanked them aside, swearing. Craning his neck in both directions, he embarked on a running commentary for his passive listeners.

'You should see what's going on, all our neighbours are clustered by the road or leaning out their windows, even Madame Dupré, I'll give her a wave, shall I? That little scamp of Pierre's is standing up on the ledge – someone will give him a shove if he doesn't watch out. There goes Monsieur Boileau, limping along at such a pace you'd think a mad dog was after him. I can see Father Benoît, no, it's not him, must be that new priest from Médavy. He's stopped to have a word with some old boy, must be from his parish, don't recognise him. The old folk can't resist being part of the action, can they? And look, Lucette, there's your friend Yvette with her son Julien, it must be him. Showing his face at last, now that the Germans can't get hold of him for Obligatory Work Service.'

She sighed over her task, set the darning aside. Impossible to shut out the world any longer, to close her ears and eyes. But there was Thérèse, shifting uncomfortably, restless again.

'Maman, have a look for me. . .down the road,' she murmured, 'Laurence . . . can you see him?' She drew in a rasping breath. 'He said he . . . coming today, I'm sure he did.'

Calming her with a few soft-spoken words, she found a niche by the window. The street was brimming with excited townspeople moving back and forth as they called out greetings, forming clusters of eager discussion, gesticulating, arguing. A gendarme came along with a whistle, trilling shrill blasts and waving his arms about, in a frustrated endeavour to herd the crowd back towards the edge of the road. After that, the postman had his turn. He stood on a bench, sweat trickling down his face, megaphone poised.

'They're at the top, now, I tell you, move back, make way, before a truck rolls over you! *Allez, allez*! Give our friends a fine welcome! Even if they are a bunch of Yanks,' he couldn't resist adding.

The crowd struggled back, laughing, then surged into the road again. The sound of cheering drifted down from the square, drums struck up an uneven rhythm. Rising above the tumult, she could pick out the strains of *La Marseillaise*.

No sign of Laurence. It wasn't like him to let any event delay his visits, but this was something he could never have anticipated. Shielding her eyes from the glare, she scanned each group passing by, hoping to catch a glimpse of Laurence chatting with friends, willing him to emerge from the crowd with a smile on his face, sauntering towards them.

Now came a piercing whoosh of whistles in a cacophony of cheers, shouts and screams of jubilation. The first two convoy trucks emerged from clouds of dust, engines throbbing and spluttering, soldiers waving good-naturedly at the enthusiastic crowd. They seemed to be wearing the same pudding basin helmets as French troops, though some of these were encased in a kind of mesh; their uniforms a muddy shade of green. The trucks juddered to a halt, then moved on at a crawling pace, while the crowd streamed round them.

Lucette was completely mesmerised by the scene beneath her. The crowd surged and swayed, arms flailing, pelting the cars and marching soldiers with rose petals, marigolds and daisies, hastily cropped from gardens, even sawdust confetti from workshop floors.

Nadette and Jeanine were elbowing through the crowd, making towards one of the convoy trucks. They tried to scramble up, shrieking and laughing as they tumbled back again. Soldiers leaned from the truck to shout encouragement, reaching out to haul them aboard. There was a chorus of cheers and wolf whistles as the girls threw their arms around the soldiers, before falling back.

Madame Dupré was in her window across the road, hurling streamers with abandon. Had she been hoarding them all this time, Lucette wondered, waiting for this day of all days?

From the sickbed, the racking cough started up again. Lucette stepped back, filled with compunction, her eyes moving from Thérèse to Albert, still intent on his window vigil. She tugged at his sleeve.

'There's too much dust coming in, Albert. Could you please close the window now, it's not good for her.' She moved over to the bed, digging in her pocket for a handkerchief.

Albert turned round with evident reluctance, viewing his daughter as if taking in her presence for the first time. His eyes gleamed as they lit on the champagne bottle on the bedside table, the glass set beside it. 'Ah! Time for your medicine! A perfect day for it,' he announced, waving the bottle at her.

'She's already had a dose, Albert.'

In a state of oblivious elation, he grabbed the glass and poured a foaming stream into it. 'Come along, Thérèse, let's have a toast! To the Liberation! To the end of the Occupation! Drink up now, that's the spirit.' Thérèse offered a weak smile, eyes brimming with tears, as he thrust the glass beneath her quivering lips. Albert spilled half the contents down her chin before he abandoned the attempt, draining the glass, tossing it to the foot of the bed. Muttering under his breath, he rushed over to the armoire, wrenched both doors open and started burrowing inside. With a grunt of satisfaction, the champagne crate was hauled out and pulled over to the window. Lucette stared, bewildered, trying to fathom his next move. No use trying to stop him when he got into these states.

One of the convoy trucks was rattling and choking just below the window. The driver toyed with the throttle, soldiers crowding the open platform. Albert leaned out the window, waving the bottle at them.

'Here you are lads', he shouted, popping a cork into the air. The foaming Champagne spurted an arc over their heads. The soldiers gaped at the window, forearms raised, expletives turning to laughter when they realised what Albert was doing. The tallest one made a lunge for the outstretched bottle and poured a stream into his mouth, eyes gleaming.

'Hey, Jimmie, get a load of this, it's champers, mate, the real fucking stuff. Hurry up, man, the stuff is fizzing like a grenade.' His comrade wasn't slow to respond. 'Over here, pal, let me take it off your hands before it explodes.' Roars of laughter and a wave of the bottle to Albert as the truck juddered into motion again.

Albert began popping corks compulsively, passing fizzing bottles out the window, pouring libations into outstretched helmets, shouting and gesticulating to anyone whose attention could be captured.

The familiar whine of aircraft sounded amidst the din of the street. Lucette repressed a shudder. Sitting on the edge of the bed, she took up Thérèse's hand, fondling it, murmuring words of reassurance as the tumult in the street continued unabated. 'Nothing to worry about, it's one of ours, ' Albert told them. Above the din in the street they heard the back door slam, pounding steps on the stairs. Laurence was with them at last. His chest heaving, visibly shaken, he rushed to the bedside, taking hold of Thérèse's outstretched hands, kissing her cheeks in desperate fervour.

Pulling himself away, finally, he subsided into the chair beside her, delving into his pockets, wiping his brow with a crumpled handkerchief. Lucette stared in consternation at the pallid face, the glazed eyes.

'I've just had a narrow escape,' he announced. At these words, even Albert turned round, bottle in hand. Thérèse began to tremble, tears rolling down her cheeks.

'Just listen to this. I was at home getting ready to come round to you. I'd put on a clean blue shirt, and there I was, right by the door, leaning over to lace up my boots. Someone was passing, so I glance up and what do you know there's this bloke with a rifle aiming straight at me. Can you believe it? I manage to shout out "Hey what do you think you're doing"? So he lowers the rifle, has a laugh, telling me it was lucky I shouted out, he'd taken me for a German soldier in fatigues. My shirt was exactly the same shade of blue.'

He made a ball of the handkerchief, squeezing it with both hands. 'If I hadn't seen him, if I hadn't said anything, I'd have been dead, right?' He fixed his gaze on Albert, as if expecting confirmation. Lucette crossed herself rapidly while Thérèse burst into tears, collapsing against the shoulder of her beloved.

Albert stood firm, shaking his head, the expression on his face transformed from ironic tolerance to muted respect. Stomping across the room, he presented Laurence with the champagne bottle. 'I think you deserve a drink after that!'

# Raid

The kitchen window was still open when the noise began, a muffled rumble reverberating in the darkened sky. It sounded like cascading timber at the sawmill, outsized dominos crashing to the ground in a rhythmic chain reaction. Her pulse racing, she picked up the sound of rattling retorts, the battery argument of machine guns responding to aircraft fire, the wail of planes. Heavy vehicles rumbled down the Grande Rue.

She pushed the window shut and drew the curtains, as if to obliterate the sounds coming through. This shouldn't be happening. Hadn't they just finished celebrating their liberation? All that champagne Albert poured out the window, what was it for? Another crash, followed by engines revving up, more rumbling. She tripped over a bucket, stumbled to the kitchen door. The children! Would there be time?

Albert was clomping downstairs, Claude barely contained in his arms. He shoved the squirming bundle towards her.

'He's wet through, the little horror. Get down to the pond with him, under the trees, well away from the road. I'm going back for Thérèse.'

'Wrap a blanket round her, Albert and take care, for the love of God!' Claude was wailing. Clutching him in her arms, she cried out, in sudden panic, 'Nicolas?'

'He's gone already! Bedroom window wide open, didn't you hear the shutters banging?' Heading upstairs, he called back, 'You'll find him at the pond, with the others, where else would he go? Tell him he's due for a thrashing next time I get hold of him.'

Lucette clasped the little one to her chest, hushing and soothing him, one hand struggling to peel the soggy layers off. At a time like this, she really missed the pragmatic efficiency of Francine. If only she could have stayed at home! She grabbed a shawl from the back of the door, wrapping it round Claude on her way out.

The garden path was a thin grey streak dissolving into shadowy undergrowth. Blackcurrant bushes, tomato plants, random nettles formed a conspiracy to hinder her progress, but at least the gate was open.

Crossing the lane, the darkness pulsed with the full weight of potential exposure. She was trapped, threatened on every side. Treading carefully, clutching a subdued Claude in her arms, she made her way alongside the hedge to follow the sloping path to the embankment.

The flare of distant explosions cast flickering lights on the cluster of ash and willow trees by the pond. Lucette soon found herself surrounded by a gaggle of over-excited, hysterical children, the women making ineffectual attempts to restrain them. She stepped aside to avoid stumbling over a whimpering child clinging to her mother's skirt, only to collide with the dark form of someone approaching from the same direction. Clémence grabbed her arm. 'Lucette! Here at last. Thank God for that, we were beginning to. . .'

'Have you seen my boy? Nicolas?'

Clémence waved vaguely towards the embankment. 'Just over there, he was, last time I spotted him. She held out her arms. 'Come, let me take your little one while you have a look for him. He'll be fine with me.'

Lucette skirted round the scrambling feet of Xavier and Felix as they tumbled over each other, oblivious of the too-close-for-comfort explosions. From the top of the embankment, a flash of light revealed the unmistakable silhouette of Nicolas, perched on an upturned bucket, craning his neck towards the sky. Waving his arms, he was utterly absorbed in mimicking the action taking place somewhere above and beyond them. She dragged him back, ignoring protests, confining him to a restricted view through a gap in the hedge. The kitchen door was just visible if you looked closely. Where was Albert?

It was Laurence, who staggered into view, Thérèse in his arms. Albert tailed close behind with an armful of blankets. The sky was humming, throbbing with aircraft.

'Come on, Laurence, you can do it,' Nicolas shouted. His words evaporated in the renewed cacophony of the heavens. Laurence and Albert crouched against the laundry room, sheltering Thérèse between them. Lucette grabbed hold of Nicolas, pulling him close. They huddled under the hedge. Planes roared directly overhead in an outburst of crossfire, finally tailing off in a distant drone of protest. Silence fell over them like a soft blanket: warm, reassuring.

Next to the laundry room, shadowy forms began to stir, slowly moving towards them. Lucette breathed a sigh of relief, releasing Nicolas, who darted off in search of his friends. She followed close behind. Under a willow tree, Marie and Albert were spreading blankets out on the rough grass. Laurence lowered Thérèse onto the improvised bed. He took her hand, murmuring words of reassurance, while Marie tucked a blanket round the fragile form. Thérèse had eyes only for Laurence, her gaze transfigured, radiant, apparently oblivious of the

132

perils she'd been subjected to.

Lucette swallowed the sobs of relief welling up, stilled the urge to rush over and embrace her daughter. She contemplated Thérèse with a sense of humble admiration. So young, and already the full force of love. Innocence, trust, fidelity: how could a relationship survive on any other terms?

She turned away, gazing at the night sky. A sliver of a moon, with only the promise of a star faintly glimmering.

Somewhere in the darkness, the wail of a child. It was time to relieve Clémence; Claude would be needing her.

# Aftermath

She sat at the kitchen table, absently sipping a cup of chicory coffee. Albert sawed a chunk of yesterday's bread, speared it on the edge of his knife, offering it across the table. 'Better than nothing,' he said, 'keep your strength up.' She complied, dipping the stale crust into her drink. She wasn't hungry, but refusal wasn't an option.

The sudden hammering at the door was sharp as hailstones on a tin roof. Lucette's crust slipped from her fingers, sank into the cup. Albert waved a cautionary gesture, scowling, intent on the sounds outside. Were the Germans still here after all?

'It's only me, are you all right?' A familiar, reassuring voice. She let her breath out.

Albert was fumbling with the lock. 'Hold on, hold on, give us a chance to open up.' The door swung to, releasing a flood of light into the kitchen. Flagstones gleamed like polished pewter, pots hanging from the ceiling cast a silver glow, softly swaying in currents of warm air.

Pierre greeted Lucette with a ceremonial kiss on both cheeks, clasping Albert in a heartfelt embrace, with palpable relief. 'I was just coming round to make sure you were back on track after all that palaver last night.' His eyes roamed round the kitchen, registering surprise. 'Looks as though I needn't have bothered.'

Albert gave him a hearty clap on the shoulder, simulating the assurance he seemed to think Pierre expected of him. 'Thanks anyway, old boy! Quite an adventure, wasn't it? We were almost beginning to enjoy our bivouac under the stars.' He pulled a chair out. 'Come on, sit down, have a coffee with us; give us a full report. Perhaps you'll be able to tell us what this latest dose of fireworks was all about?'

Lucette moved over to the stove, pouring out another cup of the chicory brew. How strange it seemed, going through the motions of offering hospitality, moving about in her kitchen as though last night's ordeal had never happened; Albert, true to form, making light work of a crisis.

Just before dawn, it must have been, when they finally got back to the house. Thérèse was still asleep, bless her; Claude whimpered and fussed at first, but quickly settled down for a morning rest. As for Nicolas, the lad was so exhausted that he hadn't yet stirred from his bed.

Pierre was working himself into a state of highly charged excitement as he recounted the events of the past twenty-four hours. Leclerc

134

managed to chase the Boche out of Alençon, he told them. American forces were attacking Argentan, trying to capture the Panzer divisions holding the town. As for last night, he'd heard it was all provoked by the RAF, chasing the Germans. 'English planes', he added, catching her look of blank incomprehension, 'though we weren't to know that!' It sounded worse, because of the crossfire, he insisted.

One of the RAF planes, a Lancaster, burst into flames, crashing down near St. Christophe. He lowered his voice. 'There were no survivors. Leclerc's armoured columns have been moving through the forest since then, flushing out the Panzers. I've heard. . .' He glanced at Lucette, evidently wondering whether to continue. She gave a curt nod.

He took a deep breath. 'Menier tells me there was a right set to over at Le Cercueil yesterday, just before dark. One of the columns came up against some Panzers at a crossroad. A Sherman took a hit, three of Leclerc's chaps trapped inside it.' He paused, choking silently. 'Blasted to bits, they were.'

Albert whistled under his breath. 'Jesus, what a way to go.' He shook his head, repeatedly.

Lucette turned away, making the sign of the cross, silently articulating a prayer. Would it ever come to an end, all this death and destruction?

Albert was posing questions, again, relentless in pursuit of further details. 'Which crossroad was it? What happened to the Panzers? Were they the bastards ploughing up the Grande Rue last night?

Pierre spread his hands with a shrug. 'That's all I know about anything, you'll have to ask Menier. I tell you, it's chaos out there, what with the Americans pushing in from the East and our chaps heading towards Argentan. I've heard reports of one hell of a confrontation over at Croix de Médavy, yesterday, quite late it the day it was; how they managed to tell each other apart God only knows. Captain Brandet, remember him, the chap we met a couple of nights ago at Odette's? He managed to pull through with his lot, probably heading for Francheville, now.'

'Good for him!' He was the right sort, he was.' Pierre's face brightened. 'At least I can tell you where Leclerc has pitched up; you'll find his headquarters just along the road at Fleuré.'

Albert nodded, 'It's the highest point, makes sense, doesn't it?'

'There's another division of Leclerc's around here,' Pierre continued, 'led by a chap called Warabiot, if I've got it right. His division stopped in Vrigny overnight, but they're heading towards Ecouché now.'

'Looks like Ecouché is going to see a bit more action, then. What about Argentan, though? Do you think the Americans have got any idea how to root those Panzers out?'

'The Boche are digging their heels in there, the Yanks can't make them budge, not yet, anyway.'

Albert shook his head, knowingly. 'If they've got any sense, they'll circle round Argentan and squeeze the buggers out.'

'Never thought of that. Obvious, though, when you think of it, if the Canadians are pushing down from Falaise. We'll find out soon enough.' He drained his cup as he got to his feet. 'Best I get a move on, don't want to make myself into target practice for a stray Hun, do I!'

She was clearing the table a few minutes later when Pierre popped his head through the door. 'Me again! I think Laurence is on his way to see you – give him my best wishes, won't you? Clémence tells me he was quite a hero last night!'

Laurence stumbled through the entrance soon afterwards, nearly tripping up on the doorstep. His face was an ashen shade of grey, the eyes bloodshot. Without appearing to register Albert's greeting, he slid down onto a bench by the door, staring at the ground. After a few moments, he buried his face in his hands, shoulders quivering. Sobs broke from him.

Albert shifted his feet, contemplating the flagstones. Lucette crossed over to sit next to Laurence. At least she could be there for him in his distress, whatever had caused it, without intrusion. She ran through the gauntlet of potential catastrophes, a burning knot tightening in her chest at the thought of what might have happened. It was all she could do to stop herself taking Laurence by the shoulders to shake him, entreat him to speak, to tell her it wasn't Marcel. Think of this poor lad, look how he suffers, she reprimanded herself. She rested an awkward hand on his arm. The sobbing subsided into sniffs and gulps. He accepted the proffered handkerchief, sitting upright, now, his unfocused gaze on the wall.

'I came to tell you . . . Papa. . . ' Lucette drew her breath in, at once relieved and shamed.

In a choked voice, Laurence managed to force the words out. 'He's. . . dead.'

There was a long silence. Laurence seemed to collapse into himself. Lucette drew back, feeling the impotence of her sympathy in the face of such sudden loss.

'They tried to save him,' Laurence blurted out. 'American troops.

136

They put the stretcher in a command car, drove him all the way to Le Mans.' His eyes met hers. 'Marcel was with him. He stayed with Papa until the end.'

Lucette nodded, lowering her gaze. She could picture Marcel in the command car at his father's side, remonstrating with the driver, protesting at every pothole. He would have made desperate efforts to rally his father, talking incessantly, cajoling him back to consciousness, begging him to utter just one word.

Albert pulled out his *tabac gris* from a back pocket, rolled up a cigarette, fingers fumbling. The task accomplished, he hesitated, then rolled up another one, offering it to Laurence, who shook his head. In a voice so subdued that Albert had to lean towards him to make sense of it, the account began to emerge.

'When the Yanks came through town, do you remember how they pushed on towards La Petite Marigny, driving the Germans out without too much of a struggle?' He glanced at Albert, waiting for his nod of confirmation. 'Monsieur Vallon, our neighbour, was elated with the news, he uncorked a bottle of champagne straight away, inviting Papa and a couple of his friends to come and have a glass. They soon realised that their little party was a bit premature,' he added, in bitter tones. 'More Huns turned up, possibly strays who'd been holed up in the château, we're still not sure. Papa and his mates heard the gunfire, panicked, thought they'd better get back home.' He thumped his leg with a fist. 'If only they'd stayed put, they'd have been all right.'

'They weren't to know, though, were they,' Albert said, in a vain attempt to reassure him.

Drawing breath, Laurence continued, doggedly. 'It happened while they were running back across the field just behind Vallon's house. Some Yanks were coming along the road where it runs alongside the field. They caught sight of Papa, Monsieur Vallon and his friends, took them for Germans on the run, opened fire.' He cast a bleak look towards them. The ones who could run faster got away.'

Albert seemed to be struggling to find the right words. 'A terrible business,' he pronounced, shaking his head. 'You'd think they would have been able to tell the difference between us and them! Bloody obvious, it should have been!'

Laurence gave a snort. 'Remember what happened to me on that very same day, the day I nearly got shot at?' He glared at Albert, accusingly. 'It's the same bloody cock-up: Papa and his mates were still in their blue overalls, the same colour as those blasted fatigues for the Boche to wear when they're off-duty.'

'*Nom de Dieu*!'

Laurence pressed his arms into the bench, clenching and unclenching his fists. He gave an abrupt parody of a laugh, his voice pitched high.

'You know what they said, those Yanks, when they were trying to apologise? You know how they thought they'd explain it?'

He waited for Albert to meet his eyes. 'This has got to be the understatement of the year, this one. They called it 'friendly fire.''

There was nothing to be said. Lucette was the first to move, picking up her shopping basket by the door, setting it down again. 'I'm going to go see your Maman,' she announced, in decisive tones. The door clicked shut.

# SEPTEMBER 1944 – JANUARY 1945

# The Clearing

Marcel stood in the clearing, senses on alert. The rustle of beech leaves in the wind, branches stirring, pigeons cooing: that was all he could hear. A branch tumbled to the ground in front of him. He stripped it clean as he moved forward, using it to whip aside the brambles trailing across the overgrown clearing. The woodshed looked as though it had been pillaged since his last visit: a gaping hole where the door should have been, splintered wood hanging from rusty hinges showing evidence of hasty removal. The wall on one side had collapsed, shedding broken bricks and crumbling mortar in a cascading heap. Broken roof tiles lay scattered over the remnants of a cache of logs; hornbeam and birch, it would have been. The axe-scarred stump was still in the same place, none the worse for wear. He pulled his jacket close, turned the collar up before sinking down on it, rooting himself. He had all the time in the world, waiting for her.

There were plans to be made, he reminded himself once more. If they could manage to get away from this place, they'd be able to start a new life together; it must be possible. Paris was out of the question – that uncle of hers with the hotel would be able to track them down, but he could chase up some of his contacts in Le Mans, or even Bordeaux. He'd find more work as a typesetter with some printing firm or other, or try some of the vineyards, if nothing else. With the whole country trying to get back on its feet again, there'd be no shortage of work.

The pragmatic elements of the plan posed certain irrefutable difficulties. His brow furrowed. Would she insist on taking the little one with her? He sighed with resignation, recognising that she probably would. What about that older boy of hers, Nicolas? Surely he could stay with his aunt; he spent so much time there anyway, it could hardly make a difference?

He began to reflect on Albert, anticipating the bitter recriminations he'd be forced to endure from his old friend. All of his worst suspicions confirmed, Albert would perceive the relationship with Lucette as the ultimate betrayal, with good reason. He would be furious, desperate, perhaps vengeful.

His mind continued to revolve around the upheaval to be set in motion. Albert would have to manage, what else could he do? Sometimes that's just the way it happens. Francine would probably move back home to help out; she'd be only too pleased to be left in charge. And Thérèse would have Laurence at her beck and call once she was up and about again. Surely she would recover soon?

A beetle was navigating a cautious path through the dead leaves and bracken he'd trodden underfoot. There's always a way to overcome obstacles, he thought, watching the busy creature tunnel into a mound of leaves, to emerge on the far side.

He started up, hearing the soft crunch of pine needles, branches whipped aside in the rapid passage of someone with no time to spare. She was making her way across to him now, glancing over her shoulder as if in flight, soon to be captured. She shivered in his enfolding embrace. He felt her body begin to yield, melting into him. The next moment, she was twisting in his arms, struggling to release herself. She stepped back, clutching her arms as she shook her head. She met his eyes.

He knew at once what she was going to say.

# The Sickroom

Laurence peered into the dimly lit bedroom, hesitated, listening, as he tried to detect signs of movement. She was awake this time, fitfully stirring, constrained by the coarse woollen blanket drawn up to her chest, pulled taut on all sides. Her head rolled towards him, eyes slowly unveiling, a faint touch of colour dusting white cheeks. Cracked lips began to form the shape of words, as if in speech or prayer.

Before he reached the bedside she was overtaken by a fit of coughing, hoarse spasms racking her emaciated frame. Laurence pulled a chair up, gazing at her in alarm. He wondered whether he should call Lucette? Keep calm, she'd told him, don't do anything to agitate her. Now that Thérèse had seen him, leaving the room was out of the question.

The cough gradually subsided, her eyes were closed. He drew up a chair, sat back in it, crossed one leg over the other, then back again. He slid a hand into his pocket to check for the pouch of *tabac gris*, he was longing for a smoke. A sickroom was no place for a man; best to say good-bye and get out. He glanced at the prostrate form in the bed. The sound of her hoarse, rasping breath filled the room, a miasma of accusation, plunging him into fear and self-loathing. He turned his head away, ashamed at his cowardice.

'Laurence.'

The voice was barely audible, a pale attenuation of his name. Enough to grip his heart. He studied his feet, suffused with remorse.

'Laurence.'

He raised his head, to take in the limpid gaze, resting on him. He managed to produce a reassuring smile as he leaned across, folding his hand over her restless fingers.

'I'm here, Thérese. Right here.'

# Moving On

He strolled into the workshop, whistling under his breath, ignoring the jangling bell with as much contrived ease as he could muster. Calling out a greeting, he continued into the room, then stopped, abruptly, the whistle petering out. Up-ended saddles, a tangled heap of harness and bridle, reins, buckles and collars, strewn across the floor. There must be something wrong. Was it vandalism, one of Albert's clients, gone off the rails? Could Nicolas have got himself into one scrape too many? He drew his breath in. An excess of grief? Thérèse? Had she. . . He dismissed the thought as soon as it came; Laurence would have told him, he visited nearly every day.

A quick glance towards the workbench reassured him. There was Albert, settled in his usual place on a high stool, intent on stitching a harness, or something of that ilk. The familiar smell of tarred thread wafted towards him.

Surveying the disordered heap strewn across the room, Marcel felt his chest contract once more. There was only one other possible excuse for this. He clamped his teeth together, his jaw rigid. Albert knows, beyond a doubt. Typical of the old boy that he should find out, now that his relationship with Lucette had come to an end. The fact that it was over wasn't going to make his task any easier. Swallowing saliva to ease his dry throat, he forced himself to make the first overture.

'How's it going then, Albert? Not short of work at the moment, eh?'

A wall of silence absorbed his words. Albert didn't look up. What could he say to break the silence? Perhaps he could ask about Thérèse? The words died on his lips. Marcel shifted his feet, cleared his throat, fixing his gaze on the rolls of cowhide in the corner. He'd try once more.

'I might be going to Rennes to pick up some work. My boss tells me there's an opening at their other branch. He thinks I should take it up.'

Albert's glove encased hand wavered in mid-stitch, steadied and carried on. At least he can hear me, Marcel noted, reading it as a sign to continue.

'Typesetters get more hours there and the work should be varied. They do Almanacs, bank notes, things that people actually want to use.'

Still no response. Marcel kept up a hesitant flow, a note of desperation entering his voice. 'There's more of a future for me in a larger firm, I'm sure. Old Monsieur Dambert wants us to specialise in religious tracts from now on, he's setting up an outlet at Lisieux. I really can't see myself coping with that sort of thing!'

He heard a muffled grunt from the hunched form on the stool. Albert took another long, painstaking stitch and tied a knot, cutting the thread. Lifting the harness, he gave it a shake before setting it on the workbench. He sighed, pulled his gloves off and stretched his fingers out, cracking the knuckles. His eyes stared into space, then shifted towards the door.

'You'd best be moving on, then, whatever you decide to do,' he said. 'Musn't stand in your way. No indeed.' Leaning over, he picked up the harness again, intent on inspecting the repair.

Marcel flinched, took a couple of steps towards him. There must be something he could say. The bent figure was absorbed in his task, the rounded back impenetrable. It would be a futile attempt. At the door, he turned round. A few parting words would be in order, it was the least he could do.

'Right then. See you sometime, perhaps when I come over to visit my mother. Goodbye for now.'

There was a murmured response of some sort, he thought, although he could have imagined it. Albert sat motionless on his stool, staring at the wall. The harness was slack in his hand.

# Loss

Moving awkwardly in the confined spaces of the darkened bedroom, she groped her way to the mantelpiece, lit the candle. The statue of St.Thérèse emerged from the depths, glowing, generating a sense of warmth in the cold damp space. With economic, unhurried movements, she drew the curtains back and opened the window. The outside shutters creaked as she released the latch. With winter coming on, there was only just enough daylight in the afternoon sky to air the room and make sure that everything was in order.

Turning towards the bed, she smoothed out a tiny pucker in the lilac bedspread, repositioned the heart shaped embroidered night case resting on the bolster. She slid her hand into the case, fingers searching out the *broderie anglaise* trimmed collar of the cotton lawn nightgown. It remained perfectly folded, just as she had left it. On the bedside table stood a cameo portrait photo in a circular white frame. Handling it with careful precision, she wiped away some invisible dust, polished the glass. Turning the frame over she held it close for inspection, poring over the delicate hand-written inscription slanting across the back. For dearest Maman, with all my love, Thérèse. It was the day her engagement was announced, plans for the wedding were in full discussion at the time. The radiance of her expression shone through the posed formality of the studio portrait.

Lucette set the photograph face down on the table, eyes brimming with tears. She pulled out a handkerchief to wipe them, calming herself before turning her attention to the rest of the collection.

The old oak frame contained the childhood photograph she liked best: Thérèse in her school smock, hair in plaits, rogue ringlets curling round her ears, trying out a smile to oblige the photographer.

Another ornate, gold painted frame made the most of Thérèse in a white tulle confirmation dress. Lucette gave a wry smile. How she'd struggled to get it finished on time! The bouquet of white roses came from Mathilde's garden, an unexpected gesture from her preoccupied sister. Lucette gave a wistful smile, one hand stroking her distended abdomen.

Her smile faded as she picked up the last photograph, a tiny one, taken just two months ago: Thérèse propped up in bed, emaciated, sallow cheeked, eyes staring into a void. Lucette closed her eyes, unable to continue. She brought the image to her lips, replacing it with tender reverence beside the others.

Time to check the clothes now. The wardrobe door swung open without sticking this time, releasing a waft of lavender and mothballs. Everything was in place, just as she would have expected. She picked up a camisole and unfolded it, holding it to her cheek, closing her eyes, trying to invoke the presence of Thérèse in the worn soft cotton lawn, the frayed satin ribbons. It offered her no more than the lingering scent of Marseilles soap. She sighed, folded the garment, carefully, and replaced it in the drawer.

What else could she do but move on to the last task? There on the bedside table was the daily missal. Holding it to her chest, she lowered herself into the wooden chair set against the wall. Her legs were aching. The missal fell open, she decided to read whatever passage her hand uncovered.

*Out of the depths have I cried unto thee, O Lord, hear my voice, let thine ears be attentive to the voice of my supplications. If thou, Lord, shouldest mark iniquities, O Lord who shall stand. . .*[13]

She closed the book before reaching the end, her face contorted with raw distress. Surely, she had already been judged for her iniquity, this was not for her. God had seen fit to punish her for her mortal sin by taking the child she loved above all others. No amount of supplication could change that. She gazed at her protruding abdomen as if suddenly aware of some gross deformation. How could she bring another child into the world? He would surely take this one too?

She set the missal aside, trembling hands pressing into her pain ravaged face. Rising to consciousness came the opening words of the rosary, taunting her:

'*Hail Mary full of grace blessed art thou amongst women and blessed is the fruit of thy womb Jesus, Hail Mary full of grace blessed art thou amongst women and blessed is the fruit of thy womb Jesus. . .*'

She forced the words to her lips again and again, as if in punishment, surrendering, in the end, to the ritual incantation, taking solace in endless repetition. The candle flickered, extinguishing itself, leaving her sitting in darkness.

# Birth

She was adrift in a shifting kaleidoscope of dazzling lights, blurred forms, crying children. Sharp cords pulled tight through her lower belly, pulsing, throbbing, anchoring her to the bed. Keep still, she told herself. the pain will ease off, ebb away.

A looming shadow cut across the light, coming in close enough to smother her. It reminded her of bundles of laundry in the arms of German soldiers: shirts, trousers, socks rolled up, thrust towards her at the kitchen door. She turned her head away, flinching; no, she was too tired now, another time, another time.

Just one child now, plaintively wailing, someone should attend to it. She closed her eyes.

An insistent voice broke into her reverie. 'Come now, Madame Griot, look, here's your little girl, a present for the New Year.' The beaming face of the midwife came into focus. She was leaning towards her with a well-wrapped parcel. An angry doll's face emerged, eyes screwed tight, fish mouth gulping. A thin wail rippled the space between them. Lucette felt a tingling warmth penetrating her weakened frame. Her new born child, not taken from her. 'God be praised', she murmured, closing her eyes in gratitude, opening them again to confirm the reality of her vision, gazing at the miracle of her baby.

'Isn't she a sweet little darling? But very hungry, that's for sure,' the midwife was saying, 'Best not to go to sleep, again, just yet, *ma chérie*. If you could hold her for a moment while I plump up these pillows, then we can settle her in for *le petit déjeuner*, yes?'

The little creature seemed to find her way without much prompting, a tiny hand emerging from the bundle to cling to her breast. She marvelled, again, at this little wonder of life, the strings of attachment pulling hard.

Somehow, she dozed off again, waking to find the baby asleep by her side. She studied the minute features, anxiously, looking for evidence of paternity. How would Albert respond to her? If only he would stay away, at least until she regained her strength.

She could hear the midwife downstairs with Francine, her intonation gradually rising, taking on a raw edge of indignation as the exchange became loaded. Albert's voice interrupted, trying to placate them both, no doubt, as the sounds drifted towards the front of the house. The street door slammed shut. A torrent of inarticulate abuse filtered through the

147

floorboards, Albert admonishing, Francine shrill in self-defence, the confrontation finally trailing off into silence.

It came at last, the stomp of boots on the stairs, every step driving a wedge through her. Lucette squeezed her eyes tight shut, pressed her hands together. 'Mary, mother of God, I implore you, be with me in my trial,' she whispered, 'Thérèse, blessed saint, protect me, save me.' Distress stirred her to more desperate measures. 'I promise to make a pilgrimage to Lisieux every year, to offer thanks to you in my daily prayers. I swear, by all the Saints, to devote myself to you, in full gratitude, for all the days of my life.' The luminous image of the Saint came into focus. She had the face of her daughter Thérèse.

The bedroom door creaked open. Lucette stilled her trembling limbs, tried to relax her features, feigning sleep. He might not be aware that the little darling could have another father, she told herself. She looks like any new born infant, that's all he will see.

The smell of tannin and tobacco permeated the room. Albert coughed, covering his mouth, clearing his throat. Through half-closed eyes, she watched him staring at the sleeping infant, wary, but curious, gradually becoming enthralled. With cautious hesitation, he reached down, extending a hand towards the baby. The tips of his fingers brushed her cheek.

# APRIL 1947

# Revisiting

There was no trace of their meetings now. Brambles scrambled across the open space, covering the mound of debris marking the site of the shed. The beech trees had been randomly hacked, leaving uneven gaps. He turned aside, regretting the impulse to make a detour, jumping over the collapsed barbed wire fence to continue on his way. Elm trees branched high over the broad path running through the park, their pale green leaves shivering in the light breeze. Blackbirds trilled in cascading outbursts; a robin flashed across his path.

A high-pitched, excited screech broke in on his reflections. At the other end of the path, a young couple came into view, a little child between them. In the next moment, the tiny child seemed to fly, borne aloft by the adults, to be set down again some paces further along. 'More,' she cried out, 'Lily want more.'

'Are you ready, then?' The woman was willing to oblige. 'One, two, three, hup!' she chanted, as the giggling child was lifted from the ground. Down again, the little creature lost no time in demanding yet another turn, prevailing without much difficulty over any objections.

'*Eins, zwei, drei, hoop-la,*' the man intoned, the smile on his face fading as he registered the approach of a stranger.

The woman cast a casual glance towards Marcel, her gaze becoming intent as they drew close. Marcel was aware of his heart missing a beat, thumping in his throat. That chin tipped to one side, those quizzical eyes conjured up an image of Lucette. This woman was younger, though, her jaw more pronounced, the face broader. He took a deep breath, letting it out slowly as recognition dawned on him. Francine. It couldn't be anyone else. Laurence must have forgotten to mention that Francine had a child; not so surprising, with her various entanglements. Trust her to pick a Kraut for a husband! He surveyed the child with wry amusement. She certainly hadn't wasted any time.

The young couple were speaking to each other in a curious mixture of German and French. Francine stepped forward, at last, greeting him with scrupulous politeness. He knew there had never been any love lost between them.

They greeted each other, embraced, awkwardly. 'What on earth are you doing here? she demanded, as they stepped apart. He found himself slipping into the half-bantering tone she used to be able to respond to. 'I'm just passing through, really, thought I'd better show my face at home. The poor old mater must be wondering whether she's still got more than one son.'

Francine wasn't slow to pick up on it. 'About time, too, Marcel Richaud. Your brother does his best, but anyone can tell how much she's been missing you.' She beckoned towards her companion. 'Allow me to introduce you to Heinrich, my fiancé,' she announced, scrutinising his features with a wary eye, senses alert for any negative responses.

The two men exchanged cordial handshakes, complete with appropriate exchanges of pleasantries. Not a bad choice, Marcel considered, encouraged by the young man's lively, forthright manner.

During the course of the next few minutes, Marcel was regaled with a somewhat incoherent explanation by Heinrich of his internment at Damigny[14], the billeting in town, a chance meeting with Francine at the café, and workshop sessions with Albert. This was followed up with an elaborate, incomprehensible account of the interminable process of obtaining his de-mobilisation papers.

'But after all, I am most happy for everything to be late to be making encounter of Francine.' Heinrich gave Francine's hand a grateful squeeze. She met his gesture with an unexpected smile.

Marcel was more than surprised. 'Congratulations to you both,' he responded, with genuine warmth. It reassured him to find one couple, at least, willing to forget the war and get on with their lives. 'When is the happy event to take place?'

They planned to have a quiet, family gathering, she told him, adding that they were going to Mulheim immediately after the wedding to settle near Heinrich's family. She tossed her head in the direction of the church spire in the main square, just visible above the rippling line of trees. 'As you can imagine, there's not much of a welcome for us here.'

Lily had been examining some moss-covered stones by the side of the path. Now she was up again, tugging on Francine's sleeve.

'Lily want Maman, want Maman!'

'It's all right, Lily, we're going soon, give us a chance.' Francine scooped her up, settling the child on her hip as they began to stroll along.

'I won't be sorry to leave, either,' she continued, 'had enough of this place for a lifetime.'

Lily was taking full advantage of her safe vantage point to have a good look at the strange man. Marcel offered an inane grin, pulling faces, setting off a round of squeals and giggles.

'It's a good age to emigrate,' he remarked, 'she'll pick up the language in no time.'

Francine came to a sudden halt, turning towards him. 'You don't seem to understand. Liliane is my little sister, not my child. She will stay right here in her own home, with her Maman.' Absently stroking the silky hair of the child, she cast a reproving glance at Marcel. 'I should have thought you'd worked that one out by now.'

Registering his air of surprise, her eyes narrowed, as if calculating. It looked as though she was about to speak, though for some reason, she appeared to think better of it. Pursing her lips, she gave an indifferent shrug as she began to move on. 'You might be hearing otherwise in a place like this, seething with old busybodies. What do they know!'

Marcel thrust his hands into his pockets, balling his fists, his mind in turmoil. What was he supposed to have 'worked out'? That Lucette and Albert had reconciled their differences?

He felt the impact of a shaft of unreasonable, unalloyed jealousy. Scenes from the past invaded his consciousness: the fleeting pleasure invoked by a gesture, a backwards glance, the prolonged evenings of communion by the fireside, passionate encounters in woods, fields, abandoned sheds. Had it been just a passing fancy of hers, that relationship he'd thought of as irrevocable, enduring, never to be forgotten? He took a deep breath, reproving himself. What right had he to indulge in rancour and resentment? He should be happy that she had managed to get on with her life, how could he have expected anything else? With a sense of shame, he turned his attention back to Francine and the child.

Lily was squirming like a captive rabbit. She had seen enough of that man who made lots of funny faces and then ignored her. Francine set her down with a sigh, wagging a finger. 'That will do, little miss princess! I'm not going to carry you a step further.'

The prospect of an enforced march seemed a death sentence. Lily set up a wail of protest.

Marcel rummaged in the depths of his pockets for a *bonbon*, one of the paper-wrapped boiled sweets he kept on hand. 'I've got something special for a good little girl,' He squatted down before her, waving fists in front of freshly captivated eyes. Gazing at the child, taking in her dark curls, the close-set, sparkling eyes, he began to register the more significant implications of Francine's barbed comment. While his hands opened and closed in a hide and seek game, his mind embarked on a series of desperate calculations. Could this child be his own?

An impatient clamour interrupted his thoughts. Opening his fists with a feigned air of surprise, he watched her pounce on the trophy. Without further ado, she crouched down on the gravel path, blissfully preoccupied with the business of peeling the sticky paper off.

Marcel contemplated the child, his pulse beating against his skull, rebounding in his chest. Turning towards Heinrich, he offered what he hoped would pass as a smile. 'Quite an independent spirit for such a mite,' he remarked, in the off-hand manner he could scarcely hope to achieve.

Heinrich looked bewildered, but took refuge in a broad smile, nodding in agreement. It was Francine who filled him in, just as he'd hoped. 'A bit small for her age, but she's actually nearly two and a half. Old enough to know her own mind.' Her eyes measured his response.

In stunned silence, Marcel watched Liliane licking her fingers. Could this little one really be his own child? Swallowing hard, he groped for the tobacco pouch in his pocket. It was some relief to be able to indulge in the activity, to utter mild expletives as flakes of tobacco drifted from his trembling fingers.

The elm trees cast a lattice of long shadows across their path, an intricate web binding the figures beneath them. Francine was level with Heinrich, now. The two of them faced each other, brows touching, hands linked. Words of endearment streamed softly between them.

Beyond the park gate, the bell for the Angelus began to ring out. Francine stepped back, glancing at her watch. '*Tiens!*' she exclaimed, '*Allons y*! We'll never get back at this rate. Your Maman and Papa will be wondering whether we've kidnapped you.'

Lily had other plans. She scrambled towards Marcel, expectant eyes trained on his pocket.

At a signal from Francine, Heinrich moved into action. 'Come along, little *Mensch*. Oop la,' he said, swinging her up onto his shoulders. Protests forgotten, she wrapped her arms round his head, settling down for a comfortable ride home. Marcel felt his chest hollow out.

'You will walk with us?' Heinrich asked, grasping Lily's stubby legs to shift her weight. Marcel gave a shrug as he fell into step next to him. 'I might just as well.'

They passed single file through the wrought iron gates of the park, slowly moving towards the Place Centrale. Francine came to a halt, turning to face Marcel.

'You could come back with us,' she said, in level tones. 'I think that. . . Albert would be pleased to see you.' It was a guarded proposal,

153

almost a challenge, of that he was certain.

Marcel fixed his gaze on the mud-spattered gravel underfoot, the toe of his boot absently digging in. It would be tempting to accept the challenge. Water under the bridge, he told himself, taking comfort in the familiar expression. He could see himself coming into the workshop to find Albert stitching up a saddle, repairing a harness. The old boy would mumble a laconic greeting as if he'd never been away. They'd have a chat, catching up on the local news. Lucette would pop her head round the door to offer coffee. She'd give a smile, cheeks flushing, meet his eye for a telling moment before she disappeared.

He glanced at Liliane, her restless complaints transformed into giggles as Heinrich bounced her on his shoulders. If he could visit them again just as he used to, he could be the one she'd look to for a shoulder ride, for teasing games, for surprise treats in abundance. He could watch her growing up, Albert need never know.

The corner of his mouth turned down as a web of implications beset him: the deceit, the risk of discovery, the inevitable anxiety Lucette would endure, especially with Francine a party to the secret. No, it would never do.

Meeting Francine's eyes at last, he shook his head. 'Just passing through, for the moment, already running late. I'll drop by some other time.' They both knew it was never going to happen.

'Francine stepped back. 'Fair enough. They'll be sorry to have missed you, though. Won't they, Heinrich?' She linked her arm through his, in affectionate corroboration. He beamed at her in confirmation, his usual practice, so it seemed.

Marcel couldn't let himself abandon the subject on such a casual note. 'Give them my best regards, won't you? Tell them. . .' He hesitated, words failing, as he succumbed to the pressure of conflicting emotions. Taking a deep breath, he went on, 'Just tell them I'll come when I can.'

The usual ritual of leave taking took over: handshakes and token embraces accompanied by numerous expressions of goodwill. Marcel stood watching as the little group made their way across the square. Liliane turned her head, once, staring at him with absorbed interest, perhaps wondering why he wasn't coming with them. He waved, finding himself disappointed when the child turned her head away.

On the other side of the Place Centrale, a woman with a young boy seemed to be moving towards the little group. Marcel felt the blood draining from his limbs. That air of purposeful animation, the erect bearing, the brisk step, he'd have recognised it anywhere.

As if in a dream, he stared, transfixed by the scene of family reunion. The boy, Claude, it must be, raced over to Heinrich, grabbed him by the legs. Heinrich protested, good-naturedly, as he slid Liliane from his shoulders, releasing her into Lucette's open arms. Chatting together, the little group moved slowly across the square. Just before they turned into the Grande Rue, Lucette set Liliane down and took her hand. She glanced over her shoulder, as if searching for something, then stopped in her tracks. Was it a moment of recognition? She was about to move towards him, yes, he was almost certain of it. In the next moment, Liliane tugged at her hand and she turned away.

Marcel stood watching until they disappeared from sight. A chill wind blew across the Place Centrale. Turning his collar up, he set off towards his mother's home.

# 31 OCTOBER 1973

# Found

'This is what it comes to in the end,' Marcel told himself, contemplating the ranks of gleaming white tombstones, the rows of polished marble slabs like hospital beds. Sleep eternal for the citizens of Marigny in their final resting places. Ornamental plaques decorated the slabs, proclaiming family fidelity: in loving memory, in fond tribute, with all our love; perpetual tokens of irretrievable loss, positioned on top, or resting against the tombstones, as if in mutual support. There were smiling portraits of the deceased in elaborate marble frames, insistent reminders of personal identity set up to challenge the common denominator of death.

Laurence was striding ahead, turning into a path to cut across the cemetery. Following at his own pace, Marcel couldn't resist stopping to peer at the inscriptions, a novel experience for him after so many years away.

They passed a tomb aspiring to the size of a mausoleum. Corinthian half-columns framed inscriptions in elaborate orthography: Bertrand Roland Vampoule, Charles René Vampoule, Christine Eloise Vampoule. . . Marcel came to a halt. 'Hang on a moment, Laurence. Wasn't that Christine Vampoule we were talking to this morning, just outside the *boulangerie*?'

Sizing up Marcel's bemused expression at a glance, Laurence responded with mock incredulity. 'Nom de Dieu! Must have been a ghost!'

Marcel cocked his head to one side, eyeing his brother with a sardonic grimace. 'All right, all right,' Laurence capitulated, laughing. 'Take another gander, you old codger, you'll see she hasn't kicked the bucket yet!'

'Nor have I,' Marcel batted back to him, 'so watch out!' The teasing exchanges invoked a relationship of juvenile rivalry, an attempt at sibling camaraderie while they struggled to reposition their relationship. It bridged the gap between different lives, other worlds. He peered at the inscriptions again. 'I'll be damned! Never came across such a peculiar custom! Though I must say, I haven't exactly been a regular visitor to the cemeteries of Montreal.'

Laurence grinned, sweeping his arm wide. 'As you can see, the citizens of Marigny prefer to secure their last resting place in plenty of time. Especially the wife of a former mayor.' Laughing companionably, they moved on.

'The grave we're looking for is rather less ambitious,' Laurence continued, rounding the corner. He stopped short.At the far end of the path, a young woman was on her knees, crouched over one of the horizontal slabs. Praying? No. Scrubbing. The rasp of bristle against stone set up an insistent rhythm. Marcel felt his heart take a tumble, knocking at his ribs. He shot an interrogative glance towards Laurence, who nodded confirmation, spreading his hands wide in a gesture of apology. This was certainly not what they'd planned for a first meeting.

Marcel stood, immobilised, feet shod in lead. This young woman, humming quietly as she worked; she was his daughter. His own daughter.

'Bonjour Liliane', Laurence called out, 'What an unexpected surprise.' Startled, she dropped her brush, squinting at the two men, through the dazzle of morning sunlight.

'Ah, bonjour Laurence!' She flashed a welcoming smile, sitting back on her heels, pushing ringlets of dark hair behind her ears. Lucette's features, but those deep-set eyes mirrored his own. He gazed at her, mesmerised.

'Never thought to see you here on a Saturday!' Laurence was saying. 'As if you didn't have enough to do at the office all week!'

'And where else would I be if not right here, Laurence Richaud,' she chided, 'what with the Feast of All Saints'[15] nearly upon us and the family grave still unattended to? Who else is going to get round to it?' She sprang to her feet, wiping her hands on the faded blue overall, fit for purpose. 'I'm the one who tidies up here for All Souls' Day, you know that well enough. I've been at it ever since Francine went back to Germany.' She arched an eyebrow, offering a companionable grin. 'You wouldn't catch Nicolas or Claude taking their turn, not in a month of Sundays!'

Laurence expressed a degree of appreciation commensurate with her efforts, offering both cheeks twice for the ritual Normandy greeting reserved for family and close friends. Turning to Marcel, she extended a hand, warmly welcoming.

'You must be Marcel. A pleasure to meet you at last.' She hastened to brush down her overall. 'Do excuse me, here I am in my gardening clothes, hardly fit to be seen!'

Marcel could hardly take it all in. For so many years he'd rehearsed this moment, running the gauntlet of potential responses, from joyful surprise to anger and accusation. It did so little to prepare him for a meeting like this. Laurence was right; she didn't know who he was; she had no idea at all. Faced with the reality of her presence, Marcel was out of his depth, treading water, feet groping for purchase on firm ground.

'I'm very pleased to meet you. . . under any circumstances,' he affirmed, his eyes slipping away. It was a long time since he'd felt so embarrassed in the presence of a woman.

The blue overall forgotten, she surveyed his discomfort with detached interest, head tipped to one side. 'I expect it's quite a shock coming back to visit Marigny after all those years in Montreal. The life you must lead out there; Laurence has told me enough to make me quite green with envy.'

Marcel let out an uneasy chortle. 'Believe me, much exaggerated.'

Best if you break the news to her yourself, Laurence had suggested. The idea had seemed reasonable enough at the time. Now he embraced the neutral terrain Liliane had opened up.

'They're quite set in their ways, Montreal folk, very conservative by tradition. Took a bit of time for a renegade like me to get my bearings. The way they speak, for a start! You wouldn't believe what they do to the language of their mother country!'

Laurence intervened. 'You've picked up a bit of the accent yourself, you know. The way you roll your r's. . .'

Marcel chuckled, getting into his stride. 'Bound to rub off, after all those years. Give me a couple of weeks on home territory and I'll be a proper Norman again.'

'Whether that's going to be any improvement . . .' Laurence countered, teasingly.

Liliane turned towards Marcel, offering a hospitable smile. 'And how long may we look forward to having the pleasure of your company?'

He was at a loss for words again. 'It depends . . . it all depends on how things go.'

She gestured towards the family tomb, glistening after its baptism of water. 'It's kind of you to spare the time to visit Maman's grave, at any rate. I'm pleased on her behalf.'

'I'm only sorry I couldn't get here for the funeral last year,' he said, meeting her eyes for the first time. 'Still had some business to wind up.' Despite the lame excuse, he was beginning to take heart. She'd be happy when she found out, surely? Once he'd explained what they'd been through, the extraordinary circumstances, the heart-breaking decisions they'd been forced to take, she would understand, she would forgive

159

him.

Laurence had been following their exchanges with bemused curiosity, glancing from one to the other. At this point he began to edge away. 'I'll leave you two to reminisce. If you'll please excuse me, Liliane, I've got to see a man about a horse. . .'

'That old chestnut!' she countered, laughing, 'you can't fool me for a moment, Laurence Richaud.' Before he could turn his back, she added, 'don't forget to remind Sonia about tonight. Usual time, OK?' Laurence waved a thumbs up to her or perhaps to them both, giving Marcel an encouraging nod as he took his leave.

Liliane cast a critical eye over the grave. A straw basket was set beside it, crisp white chrysanthemums tumbling onto the path. 'Mince!' I've still got to arrange the flowers as well. . . ' She swooped down to gather them together, turning towards him in confusion.

'Monsieur Richaud, I hope you will forgive me, but I really must finish my little task this morning. Perhaps we could meet up for a coffee later on. . .'

Marcel had already taken possession of the scrubbing brush, eager to make himself indispensible. 'Why don't you let me finish this? You can get on with the flowers.'

'Of course not, it's very kind but I couldn't possibly let you do such a thing. Please. . .' Clutching the flowers to her chest, she made a lunge towards the brush, hoping to recapture it.

'Of course you can,' he insisted, with a teasing smile, stepping out of range. 'Please, I insist.'

Reluctantly capitulating, she surveyed him with amusement. 'You'd better roll those sleeves up, then, or you'll make a mess of that fancy Montreal shirt of yours.'

Marcel set to work, anxiety sublimated in his engagement with a novel activity. The well-worn brush resisted his first awkward strokes, but soon yielded to more vigorous application.

Liliane selected one bloom at a time, snapping off long stems, methodically setting them into a vase. 'It's so unusual to find a man who is willing to help out,' she remarked, casting an appreciative glance at him. 'Where have you been all my life?' she teased.

'Where indeed.' The brush scratched into the engraved letters carved into the stone:

Thérèse Griot, 1928 -1945

Lucette Griot, 1910 – 1971
Albert Griot, 1895 -1972

She was preoccupied with the task in hand. 'Adèle tells me I should use artificial flowers for the grave, be over and done with it, that's her view. But I don't think Maman would have cared for plastic flowers.'

'I can vouch for that,' Marcel confirmed, before he could stop himself.

She sat back on her haunches, studying him with curiosity, before picking up the next bloom. ' Laurence mentioned that you knew Maman quite well, is that so? '

He stopped scrubbing, water dripping from the brush as he gazed into space. Whether by accident or design, the conversation had come to a point where his confession could be made. 'Seize the moment', wasn't that what he'd always believed? If he couldn't tell her now, he'd never do it.

There was a lump in his throat as he managed to reply. 'I knew her well. Very well indeed.'

'Tell me more,' she urged, 'there is so much I want to know.' The last few chrysanthemums lay forgotten on her lap.

Marcel set the brush down, absently lining it up against the edge of the stone. 'It was during the Occupation. I expect you've heard quite a lot about those years, haven't you?' He cast an anxious glance at her, feeling his way.

'Not as much as you might think,' she responded, 'Maman always said she'd rather look forward than back. My father used to come out with anecdotes about the *marché noir* and his enforced duties as a guard on the railway lines. Not much else.'

Marcel cleared his throat, shifted his gaze towards the marble slab. A heap of rags lay tumbled on the ground next to it. Seizing one at random, he began to polish the stone, embarking on his account while he worked.

Nothing was left out, in the end: the friendship with Albert, his activities in the Resistance, the evenings of Belote, the developing intimacy with Lucette, her final decision to terminate the affair. Liliane proved a receptive listener, interrupting him at several points to ask searching, sometimes awkward questions. There was no evidence of the hostility he had anticipated and feared. The marble slab had acquired a lustrous sheen by the time he finished.

An hour later, they were in the café, chatting to Sonia. She brought

161

them coffee laced with Calvados, eyes sparkling with excitement with the news they'd imparted to her. Marcel cast an appreciative glance at Sonia, smiling his approval. The shy refugee child had matured into an attractive woman with a lively, sunny disposition. Laurence was a lucky man. After all those years pining for Thérèse, he couldn't have made a better choice.

From the surrounding tables came the buzz and chatter of local residents catching up with each other. The old Bakelite radio had been replaced by a bulky television, where a sitcom drama emitted an undercurrent of babble and swoon to add to the general confusion. No one bothered to look at it.

Contemplating his daughter, Marcel felt the burden of nearly thirty years slipping away. He took a sip of the coffee, letting it roll slowly down his throat. It was nectar, the best coffee he'd ever tasted. Liliane bestowed a warm smile on him.

'Your neighbours will think you've got an old man chasing after you,' he quipped.

The unexpected idea brought a flush to her cheeks. She cast a furtive glance around before the humour of his remark took effect. Turning back to Marcel, her eyes crinkled with amusement. She placed her hand on his, giving it a squeeze. 'They can think what they like. I've lost one father but now I've found another, that's all that matters.'

It was a perfect moment while it lasted. There were tears in her eyes as she drew her hand away, resting her chin on it, immersed in thought. He watched, with dismay, as her features twisted into an anxious frown.

'I still don't understand,' she said, leaning forward to level with him. 'Why did you wait all this time to let me know?'Accusing eyes pierced his skin. Marcel looked away, feeling the impact of the self reproaches he had endured for days, months, years. That last glimpse of the tiny child carried off on the shoulders of another man; he'd never forgotten it. Now, pinned down by that scrutinising gaze, he began to stammer out the excuses he had made use of for most of his life.

'I was waiting for your Maman to give me permission, basically. Laurence would have told her where I was, she knew how to contact me. Years went by, I got on with my life, she never communicated a single word.'

He picked up a matchstick from the ashtray, absently breaking it into fragments. Paltry excuses, inadequate, insubstantial, he told himself. Liliane deserved more than that.

'I blame myself for not taking the initiative when it might have been

162

possible. If I had let her know how much it meant to me . . .'

He swept the scattered fragments into a heap, aimlessly stirring. 'When she took to her bed with cancer, she asked Laurence to "guard her little secret" until Albert had passed away. It turned out to be her dying wish.'

Liliane stared into space, brooding. After a long interval, she reached for her empty cup, swirling the dregs before she set it down again. 'Maman must have thought the truth would kill him.'

Marcel felt again the immeasurable weight of betrayal. Guilt had stalked him for years; he had deceived and cheated on his old friend. An edge of bitterness crept into his voice.

'Albert had plenty of grounds for suspicion. There were indications if he had wanted to look for them. I believe he knew, in the end, what was going on, but I made myself scarce before he could bring himself to act.'

'She folded her arms, sitting back in the chair, accusation in her fixed gaze.

'I know, I know. I'm not proud of my behaviour.' He shifted his legs beneath the table. The cups rattled. Passing by with a loaded tray, Sonia cast an anxious glance at them, slowing her steps before going on her way.

'I had so many plans to make a new life with her, you must believe me. If it hadn't been for. . .'

'My brothers and sisters,' she suggested, meeting his eyes.

Marcel nodded. 'We'd discussed it, so many times. What would have become of them? Francine was independent by then, but Thérèse was still alive and well enough, living at home. Nicolas was just a young lad at the time, Claude only two years old.

He paused for a moment, doggedly pursuing his argument in the wake of her silence. 'Remember, Liliane, how much she had to lose by telling the truth to Albert. He would have turned her out, I feel sure of it. What kind of life could I have offered her? Eleven years younger, no proper occupation, no home of my own.' His eyes rested on her face, pleading. 'Your mother knew she had to keep silent. It was her only option. And that's why I kept silent too.

Her gaze began to soften. Encouraged, he let himself continue. 'At the end of the day, it was her faith that won the argument, I'm sure of that. She probably suffered terrible pangs of guilt every time we were together,' he added, in rueful tones.

'Yes, Maman was a devout Catholic, I remember,' Liliane confirmed with a heavy sigh. 'It must have cost her dearly, her relationship with you.'

He found himself unable to meet her eyes. The clamour of the café pressed in around them. At the next table, two old boys seemed to be having a discussion about the best way to breed ferrets. 'Just bung them into a cage and starve them for a bit,' the one in the flat cap contended, while his friend protested in argumentative undertones.

Sonia was in earnest conversation with a young woman, ignoring the summons of a red-faced young man in overalls, repeatedly demanding a round of drinks for his companions. He turned round to complain to them, they responded with jibes and raucous laughter.

Liliane gripped the table, the urgency of some new train of thought focusing her gaze. 'I think I should tell you that it's not completely unexpected, your revelation.'

Marcel stared at her in surprise.

'Francine dropped a few hints. She couldn't resist.' A wry smile flickered, extinguished in her next words. 'Papa might not be your father,' she'd say, 'don't take it for granted.' At first I tried to ignore her remarks, but one day, I accused her of lying. "Why don't you ask Maman about that young man who spent so much time here during the Occupation?" she retaliated, "that young man who made himself indispensible to Maman. Strange how he seemed to disappear after that." Liliane lowered her head. 'Those were questions I could never bring myself to ask.'

With a surge of remorse, Marcel took full measure of her distress. Such vulnerable innocence exposed to malicious innuendo and unprovoked revelation, all on his account.

'I'm sorry,' he said. 'I'm so sorry.' Pathetic words of apology, was that all he could offer?

Liliane gave a cursory nod. She was gazing into space, lost in reflection. 'I remember just the one occasion, some years later, when Maman might have said something. . .'

Marcel leaned towards her, expectant.

'There was a poem I had to learn at school, part of our studies on the Occupation. . . 'Let me see, how did it go?' She squeezed her eyes. 'It's by someone called Paul . . .'

'Eluard,' he prompted, his pulse racing, 'Liberty,' was that the one?'

'In the fields, on the horizon,
On the wings of birds
And on the mill of shadows

I am writing your name. . .' [9]

'That's it!' Liliane beamed approbation. 'Let me tell you what happened. I was in the front room, having a go at reciting the poem for a school assignment, struggling to recall the words. Maman came in. "Do carry on," she said, sitting down for the first time that day; Maman was always so busy. Pleased to have captured her attention, I started from the beginning again. Every time I faltered, she came in with the right word. When we got to the end, I went over to give her a hug and I could see she had tears in her eyes. She told me how she'd found the poem and kept it to show you, how you'd read it together many times. She went on to describe your evenings together when you read other poems. It opened up a new world for her.

'"He had such a lovely voice," she told me, "I wish you could have heard him reciting those poems." I was on the point of asking for more when Nicolas barged in. The moment passed.'

She shifted in her chair, suddenly restless. 'Perhaps I should have looked for an opportunity to raise the subject again, but it never seemed the right time.'

Marcel wiped his eyes, profoundly moved. 'All those years ago and she still remembered me. . .It's more than I deserve.'

Liliane's eyes filled with tears, meeting his. She seized his hand, squeezing it, before pushing her chair back. 'I must go,' she said, 'Laurence and Sonia are coming round for supper. Claude might join us too. You'll come along, won't you . . Papa?'

On his feet now, a warm glow suffused every part of his body. He was Liliane's father at last, and proud of it.

He bowed towards her with arch formality. 'I'd be delighted.'

Waiting for Liliane at the door, he watched her slow progress through the café, as a string of acquaintances laid claim to her. With good-natured solicitude, she offered advice, a few words of support, not forgetting to exchange greetings with the older residents. At last she was with him, drawing her arm through his. Anyone watching would think they'd known each other for years, he thought, stepping out with pride.

They reached the crossroads at the end of the Grande Rue. She dropped his arm, turning towards him, eyes kindling in expectation. 'We'll see you at seven o'clock sharp, then.' She kissed him on both cheeks, giving him a warm embrace.

He began to cross the road. 'Papa!' He stepped back, turning towards her.

'If you stay in Marigny long enough, I might introduce you to my new friend.'

'I hope he's someone I'll approve of,' Marcel countered with a grin.

'You won't be able to do much about it, either way,' she teased, heeling round. He heard her singing as she walked away.

## NOTES

1. '*Parlez-Moi d'Amour*' –sung by Lucienne Boyer

2. *Ouest-Éclair* – Newspaper widely available until 1943.

3. René Hardy – member of the French Resistance

4. *La Voix du Nord* –underground newspaper published in Occupied France from 1941.

5. Obligatory Work Service – *Service de Travail Obligatoire* (STO). From 16th February, 1943 all men between the ages of 20 and 23 were eligible for conscription and usually deported to Germany to work in munitions factories. Older men were subject to do any work which the Germans considered necessary within France. This included the patrol of railway lines.

6. Secotine – a glue made from fish products.

7. Stamps – Any products transported required certification. Tobacconists were permitted to issue licenses with excise stamps to authorise sales.

8. Jean Giono (1895 -1970) – novelist and pacifist. Marcel would have read his pamphlet, '*Refus d'obeissance*'.

9. 'Liberty' – '*Liberté*' – by Paul Eluard, *Poésies et Vérités* (1942) The RAF used millions of copies of this poem in parachute drops over Occupied France.

10. Curfew '*Couvre-feu*'- by Paul Eluard, *Poésies et Vérités* (1942).

11. 'Operation Overlord' – code name for the Battle of Normandy, the Allied invasion launched on 6 June, 1944.

12. 2nd Armoured Division (*Deuxième Division Blindée*) – commanded by General LeClerc played a crucial role in the Battle of Normandy.

13. Psalm 130 – King James Version

14. Damigny - an internment camp for prisoners of war located near the town.

15. Feast of All Saints, 1st November, *la Tousaint* - an occasion marked by family visits to the graves of the departed.

# GLOSSARY

*bain-marie* – a large, lidded tub adjoining the cast iron range, used to heat water or to wash clothes.

*Belote* – a game of cards

*billot* –cross-section of a tree trunk used by leather workers as a work surface.

*Bock* – a tankard of beer

*Briquet* or *Briquet amadou* – the type of home-made lighter often used during the war.

*chapeau* – a higher scoring move, whereby one disc lands on top of another.

*chaudron* – A large iron pot used for heating water and boiling washing.

*collier* –halters used for work horses, to enable them to pull heavy loads. These were padded with heavy cloth stuffed with horsehair.

*drôle de guerre* – a early part of WW2, often referred to as the 'phoney war' between France and Germany.

FFL – *Force Français Liberation*– the Gaullist resistance group in operation at this time.

*Gentil coqu'licot* - 'I went into the garden to pick some rosemary

Lovely fresh poppies, lovely fresh poppies, my ladies.'

*lavoir* – a shelter constructed next to a source of water, used by the community as a laundry facility. In rural Normandy, many households had no running water until after the 2nd world war.

*Maquis*- resistance groups operating in hiding, often joined by those who opted out of conscription, or were in danger of arrest for other reasons.

*marché gris*- bartering for commodities in scant supply was a common feature of daily life.

*Opinel* – a flick knife

*Palet sur planche* – an outdoor game in which discs are thrown onto a board, scoring according to the distance from the target disc.

*planche* – the poplar board on which the game is played

*pianiste* – the name for a clandestine radio operator used by the Resistance.

*prie-dieu* – a low seated, high-backed chair for kneeling on.

*pot au lait* – a small metal milk pot with a lid and handle.

*refractaires* – those who deliberately avoided compulsory work for the Germans.

*Relève*- the call-up for a forced conscription of men over the age of 18, usually to work in German factories.

*Requis*- another term used for forced conscription.

*Résistance-Fer* – a resistance network formed by workers from the SNCF. They played an active role in the sabotage of the railway infrastructure and rolling-stock during the period before the Allied Invasion.

*savonette* - a small, perfumed bar of soap, a rare commodity during the Occupation.

*tabac gris* – loose tobacco used for rolling cigarettes.

*Vel D'Hiv* –formally known as the *Vélodrome d'Hiver* – a bicycle velodrome in Paris where arrested Jews were taken on the 16th and 17th July, 1942, during a series of raids code named 'Operation Spring Breeze.'

9 781787 196650